FROZEN METAL

ERIC S. BROWN

SEVEREDPRESS

FROZEN METAL

Copyright © 2025 by Eric S. Brown

WWW.SEVEREDPRESS.COM

ISBN: 978-1-923165-95-3

FROZEN METAL

The Z56 was not an ordinary transport. There were only two of the massive, fortress-like planes in service. Mason almost couldn't believe it when his orders had come, figuring he'd never have the chance to fly one. Yet here he sat in the co-pilot seat next to Captain Wil Jensen The captain was a legend, known for being one of the best combat pilots in history. Mason was a bit in awe of the old man.

Captain Jensen's jaw line was hard, his face scrunched up into what seemed to be a perpetual scowl. Wild, dark hair, flecked with gray, topped his head. Eyes sharp and full of intelligence, he was staring ahead through the forward window. The clouds beyond it were gray and ominous. Every few seconds crackling lightning surged through them. Captain Jensen seemed to be really concerned by it. Mason had to agree it wasn't exactly normal but there was nothing strange about lightning in clouds at their present altitude. Besides, the Z56 was built to stand up to just about anything. Her systems were hardened, exterior heavily armored, and everything aboard had at least one redundancy in place.

They were a long way out from their destination with over an hour left before reaching it at their current speed. The ocean beneath them had changed to densely forested landscapes. Not that they could see them. Mason wished they could. He'd never flown over Alaska before and heard it was stunningly beautiful.

The flight was crazy, high level classified as was what they were carrying. Mason and Captain Jensen weren't alone on the massive Z56. Not only were there a pair of techs to keep an eye on the cargo itself but the brass had seen fit to assign an entire team of special ops guys for security. If everything about what they were doing wasn't so secret, Mason wagered there would have been a wing of F-22 accompanying them as well. It was somewhat surprising to Mason that he'd even been briefed on what the cargo was but he had been.

The cargo they were carrying was like something out of a Sci Fi movie. It pushed the boundaries of reality in Mason's mind. Aboard were six mecha combat units called Conus X2s or simply X2s for short. The things redefined the cutting edge of science in terms of combat. Each of them a walking, humanoid, amazingly agile tank with enough firepower to blast its way through just about anything. Of course, the X2s were brand new, experimental, and weren't truly combat tested yet. That's why they were being delivered to the base up here in Alaska. Mason was kind of sad that he wouldn't be sticking around to see the X2s get put through the fire. Even inside their storage charging cells, the things were impressive as hell. The X2s stood eight feet tall, all gleaming armor and giving a look of sheer lethalness. His thoughts were torn away from the X2s as Captain Jensen called his name.

"Mason,"Captain Jensen said, tearing him from his thoughts.

He looked up to see that the lightning in the clouds had suddenly developed into a full scale electrical storm. The Z56 banked hard to east, tilting sideways. Mason was sure the guys in the rest of the plane really loved that happening without any warning.

Captain Jensen stabbed the button of the Z56's intercom system."Heads up, people! We've run into a major storm and are taking evasive maneuvers to get clear of it as quickly as possible. Be warned, things could get pretty rough!"

"Better late than never, right?" Mason quipped, earning a stern snarl from Captain Jensen.

"Get your damn head in the game," Captain Jensen snapped.

"Hey," Mason started but a flash outside that was so bright his vision went white cut him off and caused him to jerk back in his seat.

"Damn it!"Captain Jensen yelled."We're hit!"

Multiple alarm klaxons were ringing. As Mason blinked his eyes repeatedly and his sight began to return, he saw the control panel was flashing with enough warnings to make it look like an overdressed Christmas tree.

Captain Jensen was struggling to keep the Z56 from spiraling out of control. They were losing altitude and dropping like a stone. It was as if whatever struck the plane shut down every single one of its main systems simultaneously. That shouldn't have been possible but somehow it had happened.

"Mason!" he heard Captain Jensen shriek."Get me some power!"

Looking at the console in front of him, Mason made several attempts to reboot key systems and bring them online again. Everything he was doing was failing. He wanted to scream, smash the controls with his fists but managed to hold himself together.

"Come on, man!" Captain Jensen roared.

Trying to get at least backup power online, Mason ran the process to bring it up one more time. It worked. Power surged through the plane. And the flickering lights of the cockpit stabilized into a dull red glow.

"Got it!" Mason exclaimed, thrilled that something had finally worked.

The Z56's fall ended as the large transport leveled out. It was too little, too late though. Both he and Captain Jensen saw the peak of the mountain top ahead at the same moment and knew there wasn't enough power to kick in the thrusters to get over fast enough.

"Oh my. . ." Mason began to take the Lord's name in vain in the second before the bottom of the Z56 made contact. Its armored hull thudded against rock, bouncing the plane upwards. The lights flickered and went out again but amazingly, the hull wasn't compromised. The huge transport rolled in the sky as its speed continued to carry it forward and then began to plummet.

There was no time to even attempt to reboot systems. Mason sat helpless. The lives of everyone aboard were in the hands of Captain Jensen. Straining so hard the veins in his neck looked as if they were about to burst, he delivered a miracle, bringing in the Z56 as well as anyone could. The belly of the huge transport slammed into the snow-covered ground evenly and it slid into the masses of trees below the mountain, tearing them from the earth and sending them flying like shattering tooth picks. The Z56 cut a wide path through the forest, battered and bouncing, until it cleared the trees. The huge transport whirled sideways, crashing into a snowbank where it finally came to rest.

****

A hand on his shoulder shook Mason roughly as a gruff voice told him to, "Wake up, damn it!"

Eyes fluttering open, Mason saw Lieutenant Lane before Tony leaned in to block out his view of everything else.

"What. . .what happened?" Mason croaked.

Lieutenant Lane shook his head in disgust. "Tony, check him out already!"

Tony was the sole medic aboard the transport. Mason felt the tips of Tony's fingers forcing his eyes open wider. A bright light blazed into them.

"He's dazed, sir. That's all," Tony said. "Give him a moment and he should be fine."

"That's better than you can say for this guy," Mason heard another soldier say.

Rolling his head around he saw that Captain Jensen was dead. Remarkably the forward window hadn't broken despite the force of the crash. Cracks ran throughout it but it had held for now. The console in front of Captain Jensen had overloaded and blown. Small fires still danced in spots on it. The soldier who had spoken hosed the still burning console with a blast from a small fire extinguisher.

Captain Jensen's head was lolled back atop his neck and beneath it a shard of metal was embedded in the center of his throat. The metal went all the way through into the captain's seat, tip, dripping red, sticking out of it.

"No," Mason sobbed, "Oh no."

"Yeah, buddy," the soldier with the fire extinguisher almost chuckled,"Your pal didn't make it. You ask me, it serves him right. The bastard nearly killed us all."

"Belay that crap right now, Brent!" Lieutenant Lane scolded him.

The lieutenant's gaze fell on him again as Mason tried to sit up straighter in his seat, fingers fumbling with his harness, trying to release it.

"Mason," Lieutenant Lane said his name and then asked, "Do you think you can tell me what happened now?"

Managing to get the safety straps of his harness loose, Mason leaned forward unsteadily and tried to get up.

Tony's hand met his shoulder, gently keeping him in the co-pilot seat.

"Easy there,"Tony cautioned him. "Just sit and try to tell us what we need to know."

Mason swallowed hard, collecting his thoughts, raking his brain to remember everything.

"We ran into some kind of atmospheric storm,"

Mason explained. "It was worrying Captain Jensen. There was just something that wasn't right about it. Its lightning was. . .odd. He shifted our course, trying to get clear of it but we got hit anyway."

"Hit?" Lieutenant Lane gawked at him. "By what? The lightning?"

Mason could see that Lane knew the lightning shouldn't have done squat to the Z56.

Nodding, Mason went on. "Yeah. It shouldn't have done anything of significance to us. This transport is armored against such strikes far more heavily than even other military planes. I don't understand it but main power was knocked offline. I was able to reboot the primary backup."

"Then what. . .?" Lieutenant Lane began to ask.

"We'd lost too much altitude. We found ourselves on a collision course with a mountain top and there just wasn't enough power to pull up before hitting it," Mason frowned. "Then we were going down, hard and fast. If it wasn't for Captain Jensen's flying, we'd all be dead right now."

Brent grunted but a look from the lieutenant kept him in line and his mouth shut.

"How long was I out?" Mason asked.

"Not too long," Tony assured him. "There were some injuries among our people I had to deal with but we made it in here pretty quickly."

"Was anyone else seriously hurt?" Mason asked,

not wanting to plainly ask if others had died in the crash.

"Only the colonel," Tony sighed. "The old man was flung into a bulkhead at the wrong angle. Broke his right leg and messed up his ribs too. As far as I can tell his lungs are okay and there's no internal bleeding."

Was there a correct way to be hurled into a bulkhead? Mason wondered.

"The colonel's injuries have left me in command," Lieutenant Lane frowned. "So with Jensen dead. . .you, Harry, and Tristan have just become the most valuable living assets onboard."

Harry and Tristan were the two techs assigned to the mission and he, Mason knew, was the only surviving pilot. The Z56 was equipped for V.T.O.L. As thus, if they could repair enough of its systems and get the main power back online, there was still hope that the big plane could rise up and fly again. That's what Lieutenant Lane had to be thinking anyway. Mason figured that was going to be pretty much impossible.

Taking a deep breath, Mason was beginning to feel better, more steady. He tried again to get up and succeeded. Tony backed off to give him room.

Brent shook his head at the sight, contempt oozing from him.

"So what's the plan?" Mason asked, filled with

a courage that he couldn't explain and came out of nowhere.

Lieutenant Lane's attention returned fully to him, a hint of anger flashing in his eyes.

"Do you have one?" Lieutenant Lane challenged him.

Mason shook his head in the negative.

"Yeah," Lieutenant Lane shrugged, "I don't either. . .yet. I'd say first up though is finding out exactly how banged up this plane is and getting everyone together to see what we can do about it. Any idea about where we've come down?"

Mason could only shake his head again. "Nowhere near the base we were heading for. That's all I can tell you until we get the nav back online and take a real look. If we can, I should say. Some systems were fired pretty badly, I'd wager."

"Figured about as much," Lieutenant Lane sighed. "You sure you're okay now?"

"I'll manage," Mason answered. His bruised and battered body hurt but he could handle that kind of pain. In that moment, he realized that Tony hadn't even offered him anything for it. That likely meant Lane had already ordered that everything on hand, including pain meds, were already being held back in case the worst happened and they all found themselves stuck here for quite some time. Mason didn't care for the thought of that at all.

****

Everyone onboard the massive Z56, except for Colonel Hatch and Tony, were absent. They all squeezed into one of its two crew rest compartments where most of the special ops troopers had been when it went down. In addition to it there was the pilot compartment, the main and secondary cargo bays, the sensor/comm. array room which was basically its CIC, and a small sickbay area. People had taken the available seats while others found themselves on the edges of bunks.

Mason could feel eyes on him. He was the highest ranking officer in the rest compartment even if he was Air Force. Lieutenant Lane was the acting C.O. officially though until Colonel Hatch was recovered enough to resume command. The techs, Tristan and Harry, were also subjected to occasional lingering glances. The four of them together were who would be deciding the fate of everyone in the compartment – the sole pilot, the only two who could maybe fix the transport to get it airborne again, and the acting commanding officer. Mason wasn't comfortable being looked at with such desperation. He was thankful not to be the one who was in charge of this meeting.

"Hey LT!" a burly solider Mason knew as Banner called out. "Just where in the hell are we?"

Lieutenant Lane shook his head, annoyed.

"We don't really know yet," Lieutenant Lane admitted.

A rumble of mutters ran through the gathered men and women.

"I don't see how that matters," Sergeant Shelby Hall forcefully shot up a hand letting Banner know he needed to shut his mouth. "What about getting us into the air again? Is that gonna be possible?"

With a heavy sigh, Lieutenant Lane gestured for Tristan and Harry to take her question.

"Well. . .Uh. . . ." Tristan stammered.

Harry took over for him. "We just don't know that yet either. We're still attempting to see just how bad all the damage is."

"And how long is that gonna take?" Another soldier, Dirk, barked.

"What about him?" Clay, another special ops guy pointed at Mason. "Is he even able to fly us out if we can fix this piece of junk?"

"This Z56 is not a piece of junk!" Tristan burst out in rage. If Lieutenant Lane hadn't moved to block him, the tech might have flung himself foolishly at Clay. His anger was that intense. Tristan didn't mind being insulted himself but he didn't let anyone talk crap about a transport as well designed as the Z56.

"Whoa!" Lieutenant Lane restrained the tech.

"Ah, let him go, sir," Clay smirked. "Teaching him a lesson would make me feel better."

"Clay!" Sergeant Hall snapped.

Clay slumped back in his seat, palms out in a show of surrender, frowning, too smart to give her any lip.

Seeing he wasn't going to be causing any more trouble, Sergeant Hall's eyes fell on Mason. "So, are you able to?"

Mason swallowed and nodded. "Yeah. Of course," he assured her. "Assuming those two can get her fixed up."

"Ahem," Dirk got everyone's attention again. "Harry, I think we're all still waiting for an answer."

Harry shrugged. "I just can't tell you, Dirk. There's a lot for us to look over and check out."

"I think it's clear that our priority, long term, is getting out of here A.S.A.P and onto the base we were headed for. Right now though, Tristan and Harry are going to have their hands full keeping the power on. The backup battery isn't going to last forever. If it goes out, we'll all be popsicles. It's winter up here. The temp out there is colder than hell and ain't going to be warming up," Lieutenant Lane said.

Sergeant Hall spoke up and took over. He let her.

"Breaking down what we've all just discussed," her gaze moved around the room, "What we need to do is let Harry and Tristan get to checking out this plane. While they're doing that Mason can perhaps figure out just where in the hell we're at and how far away from the base we are. Regardless of what Mason finds, I think we need to send out a party to take a look at the area where we have come down. And of course, we need to check over the cargo and make sure that none of the suits were damaged. Taking stock of how much food and water we've got on hand wouldn't be a bad idea either."

Mason found himself smiling at just how take charge and efficient she was. Lieutenant Lane was too.

"Sounds like we know what needs to be done," the Lieutenant nodded. "Tristan, Harry, Mason, get out of here and get to it. The rest of you yahoos hang around. The sergeant and I will be splitting you up into squads so that we can get all the rest of the crap that those three aren't handling done."

"Come on," Harry motioned to Mason and Tristan.

The three of them left, heading forward along the length of the plane.

"Let's see what we can do about getting the systems you need up and running," Harry thumped

Mason on the shoulder. "Then we'll leave you to it and get to work on making sure the power is going to stay on."

As they entered the Z56's pilot compartment Mason was startled by just how damaged it was. When he had first regained consciousness, there was a fire and some blown out, cooked control panels but that was all he remembered. Looking again now, Mason saw that the roof of the compartment was nearly caved in, cables dangling downward. They weren't sparking. Tristan and Harry already made sure of that apparently before attending the gathering they'd just come from. There was blood drenching Captain Jensen's seat and all over the floor beneath it. His body was gone. Someone had carried his corpse away. Mason imagined it was being stored in the Z56's small medical bay. That was good because he might not have been able to handle seeing it again.

Harry headed straight for the co-pilot seat, sliding onto it.

"Your controls here are all we've got to work with," he said, tipping his head in the direction of Jensen's. "Ain't nothing left over there."

"Tristan, get your butt over here and get this panel off," Harry ordered, thumping one beneath the control panel.

Mason watched them work. The two were dang

good at what they did. Within minutes navigation was back online.

Harry got up, offering Mason the seat at the control panel.

"Need anything else?" Tristan asked.

Mason shook his head. "I don't think so. I'll let you know if something comes up."

Giving a sharp nod, Harry flashed him a wry grin, "If only fixing the rest of this bird were going to be as easy as that was."

"Damn straight," Tristan agreed.

They left, leaving Mason alone in the pilot compartment. The lighting in the compartment was dim and an eerie shade of red. Mason leaned forward, sinking his head into his hands. He didn't sob or cry. His body was exhausted from stress and his mind. . .wasn't much better. Mason wanted desperately to just lay down, close his eyes, and pretend the Z56 had never crashed. That wasn't the reality of things though. He sucked in a deep breath and steeled himself as best he could.

With the navigation system online it took only moments to figure out that they were a hell of a long way from the base they'd been bound for. It would be impossible to make the remainder of the journey on foot, at least in his opinion. If they couldn't get the Z56 in the air again, their only rational choice would be to hole up where they were and wait for help to come. Communications were out. Harry and Tristan made it very clear that those systems were beyond repair without parts they didn't have. As thus, waiting for help to come was a dangerous gamble. They were nowhere near where they should be. Any rescue effort made to find them would likely be starting out in completely the wrong area. That would add time to them being found. . . if they were found at all.

Mason switched off the navigation system having gotten the information that was needed from it. Wasting power was something that none of them onboard the Z56 could afford. If Harry and Tristan couldn't get main power online, the battery backup was going to be used up fairly quickly just by keeping the plane's internal temp above freezing.

Rocking back in his chair, Mason stretched his arms upwards trying to work some of the tension out of them. While he had faith in Harry and Tristan's skills, he doubted the duo were going to be able to get the Z56 repaired enough to take flight. Mason had a feeling, deep down, that none of them were going to make it home. To his surprise, it didn't bother him too much. It wasn't as if there was anything waiting for him there. Brook had left him three months ago and his parents were long passed. Mason had no brothers or sisters. Hell, he didn't even have friends. Not really, anyway. Sure, he knew some people that lived in his building and played cards with some other pilots that lived in the area on the weekends but none of them were close. They didn't share things or even really speak to each other outside of the games. Mason's focus on his career for so long pretty much cost him everything outside of it. Becoming co-pilot of a bird like the Z56 was supposed to have been one of the best things that had happened to him so far in his life, not this nightmare that was unfolding around him. Nightmare, that was exactly what it felt like too, something impossible, something dark and oozing terror ever so slowly through the veneer of calmness and sanity, something that couldn't be escaped from. And there wasn't a hell of a lot he could do about it.

****

Weston was in command of the trio of soldiers gathered at the Z56 transport's rear door. With him were Zack and Chad. Thankfully there was cold weather gear aboard and they were all suited up in it. White camo, winter tactical combat jackets and vests. Zack, the unit's sniper, was carrying an MK22 rifle while he and Chad were armed with M4A1s. All of them had additional sidearms holstered on their hips and carried at least one grenade somewhere on their person. It didn't matter that they were in the fragging middle of nowhere, you always prepared for the worst because most of the time, something was going to tilt sideways and if you weren't ready, it was your arse that paid the price for it.

According to the Z56's partially working sensors, it was below zero outside before one even factored in the windchill. Cold weather gear or not, they were walking out into a deep freeze. Weston wasn't looking forward to it but orders were orders.

"What say we get the show on the road, boys?" Weston asked the others.

"Just how fragging old are you?" Zack mocked him. "Who the hell talks like that?"

Chad held a closed fist to his lips, stifling a laugh.

Weston glared at Zack for a second but then smiled. "Old enough to kick your arse to hell and back, Zack, if you keep that crap up."

Zack returned his smile. "Wouldn't think of it."

Activating the door, Weston felt the sudden shift in the temp around them as it slowly lowered. They hurried out, running down the ramp, into the frozen snow that crunched beneath their boots.

"We're clear," Weston said over comms as he looked around. They were surrounded by snow, ice, trees, and nothing else.

"Copy that," Harry's voice answered him before the door whined and began to rise behind them.

The trio waited until it was sealed back. Their job out here was to not only take a look around, getting a feel of the terrain in the area that the Z56 had come down in, but also to scope out the viability of hunting game if worst came to worst. That was if any game was around to be found.

"Which way we heading?" Chad asked.

"Does it matter?" Zack snorted.

"North," Weston told them firmly. "We're heading north."

He led the way as the three of them trudged away from the Z56 and headed into the sparse woods. The wind howled around them but it was too cold for the snow to be blowing. The chill of it hit them like a whip. Weston shuddered despite the cold weather gear he wore. Lieutenant Lane hadn't given any exact distance that they were to travel. Weston knew the LT was just hoping they would get a feel of things in the area that they could report to him.

Based on the position of the sun in the sky, Weston estimated that the day was near its end. There wasn't much sunlight left to them. His breath was visible before his eyes. The squad moved along silently with him on point. Well as silently as they could in fields of frozen snow. Weston thought about what sort of animals might be lurking around. Bears, wolves, foxes, caribou. . . Hell, there could even be bison. He and Chad had grown up as city boys by Zack's standards. Their tracking skills were lacking. The snow helped of course but they just didn't have the experience to catch things like Zack.

After only a few minutes of marching, Weston slowed and motioned for Zack to trade places with him. Chad remained as the squad's rearguard.

"We both know your eyes are better than mine," Weston told Zack.

The southerner flashed a mischievous grin.

The squad got moving again until Zack raised a hand, bringing them to a sudden halt. There something in the snow up ahead. Whatever it was, it was half buried in the snow and as large, if not larger, than a man.

Weston moved up to Zack's side, whispering, "What the hell is it?"

Zack shrugged and took out a small pair of binoculars, training them on the object in the snow and then gave a grunt.

"Bloody hell, sir," Zack lowered the binoculars, "I think it's a bison."

Breathing a sigh of relief that it wasn't a threat lying in wait for them, Weston nodded. "Come on then. Let's go see what killed the big guy."

As they drew closer, the size of the bison became clearer. The beast was massive, like a cow on steroids. Weston had never seen anything like it before. It appeared to be frozen solid. He stopped just short of the huge beast's corpse but Zack didn't. He went on by it, turning to look down from its other side.

"Holy. . ." Zack exclaimed, his eyes bugging.

Weston hurried to look at its other side where Zack was. What he saw shook the hardened veteran to his core. The bison's entire underside was torn open, guts spilling like purple, red-slicked snakes onto the melted and refrozen white they lay upon. Weston could see the animal's exposed ribs. Bile rose up his throat. He brought a closed hand to his tightly pressed together lips, forcing himself not to vomit.

"Whew," Zack commented. "Something got that guy but good."

It was obvious that whatever killed the bison had been feeding on the great beast.

"What do you think brought it down?" Weston asked, glancing over at Zack. "Wolves?"

"No way," Zack shook his head. "Look at its neck. Wolves would have come at it from a bunch of angles, ripping at it with their teeth. They couldn't have done this."

Weston looked. The bison's head was twisted at

an unnatural angle as if something had taken hold of the beast and snapped its neck from behind. "Frag," hee muttered, too stunned to manage anything else.

"That ain't the creepiest thing," Zack said.

"What?" Weston mumbled.

"The tracks. . ." Zack pointed at the ground around where the bison lay and they stood.

That was when Weston noticed them. There were imprints in the frozen snow, far deeper and wider than a human would leave behind. The prints looked human-shaped overall but the toes were all wrong. And no man or woman would be walking around in the cold like this. He didn't have a clue what to say. Weston just looked back up at Zack hoping the southerner might have a rational explanation for what they had just found because he sure as hell didn't.

Seeing his expression, Zack frowned. "If you're wanting an answer as to what made those and killed this bison the only one I got for you. . .you ain't gonna like at all."

Chad joined them, staring at the mutilated, partly eaten corpse of the bison and then the tracks in the snow.

"Whoa. . ." He breathed. "What the hell?"

"That's what we're trying to figure out," Weston said.

"I'd think it's fragging obvious," Chad blurted out. "A bear ripped this thing open and left in a hurry afterwards, that's why the tracks are messed up."

Zack laughed loudly. "Man. . .you're really something."

"You got a better explanation?" Chad challenged the southerner.

"Weston," Zack's voice was as cold as the air and deadly serious. "There's only one thing I have ever heard of that could do this and make those prints."

Knowing what Zack was likely about to say, Weston shook his head and said, "Don't. Don't say it out loud."

He was afraid doing so might make it real.

Chad looked at him and then at Zack. "Guys?"

"Look," Zack said. "We gotta accept what's right in front of us and you know it. Whatever snapped this bison's neck had to be humanoid and these foot prints back that up."

"No," Weston shook his head. "Don't. There's got to be. . ."

"There's not," Zack stopped him. "The thing that did this was a Yeti."

Weston would have said Sasquatch but Yeti was damn close enough.

"There aren't any Yeti in Alaska, Chad took on a

know-it-all tone. "They're an Asian thing."

"Fine," Zack shrugged. "A Sasquatch then or a Bigfoot. Whatever the hell you want to call it."

Weston was shaking his head again. "No. No. No. It can't be that. Those things are just stories. Creatures like that don't exist in the real world."

"I'm just calling it as I see it, Weston, "Zack told him.

"Uh. . ." Chad cut in. "If there really is some sort of monster out here that did this, shouldn't we be getting the hell out of here?"

"He has a point," Zack admitted. "Sure, this bison is frozen but in these temps. . .who knows how recently it was killed? The thing that did this could be out here in these trees with us. And we might never know, not unless it wants to be seen or comes at us. I mean, this is its home. We're the intruders here. It has the home field advantage."

Weston got his emotions under control, straightening up. "I don't buy it but honestly, I think we've seen all we need to out here. I'd say it's time to head back before the sun sets."

"Good idea," Zack agreed.

They'd traveled quite a ways from the Z56 and were going to have to hustle to make it back before the world was dark around them. Double timing it with Zack in the lead, they moved in silence other than the crunching sounds of their boots in the frozen snow. As they had gotten going, Zack traded weapons with Chad, wanting something that could fire faster than his sniper rifle if he ran into trouble while he was on point. The trees around them were sparse for the most part but in some places they were more clustered.

Weston couldn't shake the feeling that the others were right and they weren't alone. . . that something, not human, was out here with them. That feeling grew more intense the lower the sun sunk behind the distant mountains. Zack had been right. None of them saw the monster until it was too late.

A gigantic, white form burst from a crop of trees, roaring its rage. Zack, the poor bastard, never stood a chance against it. The southerner swung his M4A1 around but even his keen combat instincts and skill were no match for the monster's speed. It moved impossibly fast for something its size. The thing was like a white blur, batting the weapon from Zack's hands even as he squeezed the trigger. The rifle was firing as it spun away into the trees, Zack's trigger finger going with it. A hair-covered hand clasped Zack by his throat. Lifting him effortlessly from the ground as his legs kicked wildly beneath him, the monster plunged its other hand into his abdomen. It sunk deep and emerged tearing a fistful of his guts loose. Blood splattered onto the snow, staining it red. Zack's body was twitching and spasming from the pain.

Much to Weston's shame, it was Chad who got off the first shot at the monster. He'd run to obtain a better firing position to lessen his odds of hitting Zack as he targeted the monster. Chad's rifle blazed away on full auto. The stream of rounds it spat tore at the monster, spotting its white hair with widening patches of wet redness. The bullets were hurting the creature but not really penetrating deep enough to do as much damage as they should. Its muscles were so dense beneath the creature's hair and flesh that they almost served as a form of natural armor. The creature flung Zack away, roaring, and bounded towards Chad.

"Oh frag!" Chad yelped, seeing the monster coming at him. He whirled about and started running like hell.

Weston could see that there was no way in hell that Chad was going to escape the raging beast. He seemed to be heading towards a nearby tree as if planning to hurl himself up it. The thing chasing him was no pack of rabid dogs. Weston knew if it didn't follow him straight up, the thing could likely just knock the damn tree over. It was up to him to stop the beast and save Chad's butt.

Bracing his rifle against his shoulder, Weston carefully targeted the monster's head and face before squeezing the trigger. He fired in short bursts instead of on fully automatic. Each three round stutter from the gun ripped at the beast. The first struck its left ear. The top of it was blown away as another bullet hit near the opening of its ear canal. The monster staggered sideways, thrown off balance, managing to catch itself from falling over at the last second. Its body shifted, swinging in Weston's direction but he was already firing again. The second trio of rounds all punched into the beast's forehead. None of them made it through the bone there but they must have sure as hell cracked it beneath the skin. The beast was sent stumbling backwards but Weston still wasn't done. His third burst was aimed lower as he tried to hit its eyes. He missed them as the beast flung its head back in a shriek of absolute pain from the damage done to its forehead. Instead, the bullets split the thing's upper lip and tore away part of its right nostril.

Weston's intervention gave Chad time to recover from the panic that had sent him into a mad flight. Rejoining the fight, Chad emptied the remainder of his rifle's magazine into the beast. The bullets drew more blood. The beast's rage and bloodlust was replaced by a shocked fear that something as fragile and little as them had caused it so much pain. It gave up the battle, launching itself into a desperate retreat. The beast was slower, trailing blood in its wake, but still far faster than a human could ever be as it sprinted into the woods it had come from.

Chad was busy popping his rifle's spent magazine and slamming a fresh one home. Weston, though, got off a few more bursts at the monster's back. He couldn't tell if they made contact or not but some certainly struck the trunks of the trees the monster was zigging and zagging through. Showers of splintering bark erupted from them.

Then everything was still and quiet, the beast gone.

Chad sunk to his knees. His mouth was open and eyes wide. He was in some kind of post-combat shock. Weston, figuring that Chad would snap out of it on his own, rushed to check on Zack. The southerner's body lay sprawled out in the snow, steaming red seeping out around it. Zack's eyes were closed. He was unconscious. Weston was grateful that he was. The amount of pain from his ruptured and torn guts was likely more than almost anyone could take. They were like red-slicked, purple snakes protruding from the open mess of his abdomen, some spilling down along his sides. As irrational as it might be, Weston set his rifle aside and began scooping up his fallen friend's innards and piling them atop and into the hole the beast had left in Zack's body. Shrugging off his combat pack, Weston yanked out a large bandage, pressing it down hard over Zack's exposed guts. His hands were smeared bright red with Zack's blood and other even more sickening fluids. The pain of him doing it jerked Zack back into the waking world.

Zack screamed like a banshee out of hell, his shriek so full of pain that it made Weston nearly vomit. He head swung away from the sight of his wounded friend but Weston continued to press down on the bandage. Zack's eyes rolled up to show only whites and he fell unconscious again.

"Chad!" Weston snapped. "Get the hell over here! I need help!"

If Chad heard him, he gave no sign of it.

The bandage was self adhesive so seeing it was as much in place as he could get it, Weston shot Zack up with a powerful painkiller, flinging away the spent, emergency syringe then rose awkwardly to his feet and half walked, half stumbled towards Chad, calling his name again. This time his shouts seemed to get through to Chad, at least a little. Blinking, Chad rolled his head on his shoulders as if waking up from an intense dream. . . or nightmare.

"Zack?" he croaked.

"Alive," Weston answered, "But only barely."

"That. . . that thing. . ." Chad managed to get out.

"Don't think about that right now," Weston ordered. "We've got to get Zack back to the Z56 before he bleeds out. Hell, it might be too late for him already but we have to try."

"Right," Chad said firmly, as if fully finding himself again.

Keeping a sharp eye out for the monster's return, the two of them together lifted Zack between them and got moving. The darkness around them was growing thicker as the last rays of the setting sun began to fade. Every so often, a moan like that of someone being tortured would come out of Zack. Weston did his best to ignore it. There wasn't anything else they could do for Zack out here and there was no guarantee that the monster wouldn't be coming back to finish them all.

****

"Damn it!" Harry cried, jerking away from the open panel of wires in front of him. He shook the hand that had been shocked about wildly. To make things worse, sweat was dripping into his eyes. It might be below zero outside the Z56's hull but it was hotter than hell where he was. The Z56's V.T.O.L. engines were so large that there were actually crawl shafts that led into them so that they could be worked on from the inside if necessary, even during flight, during an emergency. The heat had yet to entirely dissipate from the last attempt to fire them up. Harry wiped away the sweat on his forehead with the back of his hand.

"I'm coming out!" Harry yelled.

Tristan was waiting on him outside the crawlspace when Harry emerged.

"That bad, huh?" Tristan asked.

Harry grunted. "Worse. All the wiring is fired to hell and back."

The two of them suspected as much before beginning their work but had to try nonetheless.

"The colonel and lieutenant aren't gonna like the news," Tristan commented.

"Yeah, well, they'll have to wait to hear it," Harry said. "We've got more work to do."

"Please tell me you don't mean. . ." Tristan stared at him.

"Yep," Harry stretched, popping his back, trying to work the cramps out of his arms from working in the tight crawlspace. "No choice but to rig up a solar cell to make the batteries last at least a bit longer."

"Crap," Tristan knew it was pointless to argue. Harry was right.

The two of them headed to get geared up for the cold. Once that was done, they made their way, not to the rear bay exit, but the one below the pilot compartment. At first they couldn't open it. The door was partially blocked by snow and ice. It took a few minutes for them to work it open enough to use. Both of them were sweating from the effort as they made it outside. The cold cut Harry to the bone. It was obvious Tristan felt the same. Harry was carrying the emergency ladder that they planned to use to get up onto the top of the plane so as to set up the solar equipment Tristan was lugging along. Wiring it into the main system wouldn't be as hard as most people would think. The Z56 had been designed to make it fairly easy. The tough job was actually going to be getting up to where they needed to go. A lot of the plane's exterior was already slicked with a thin sheen of ice.

Harry began to unfold the ladder.

"Need a hand?" Tristan offered.

"Nah. I got it." Harry finished quickly and started to look for a safe place to set it up.

"Guess one of us is gonna have to hold that thing," Tristan commented.

"Yeah," Harry stared up at the wing above them. The Z56 had come down level. They didn't have to deal with any slanting.

"You brace that thing," Tristan told him, "I'll go. I'm the one carrying the solar set up anyway."

While Harry got the ladder in place as best he

could Tristan slung the solar pack onto his shoulders and made sure it was secure. They did have a replacement onboard but the things cost a small fortune. Dropping one wasn't something Tristan wanted to answer for if they got out of this mess.

"It's as good as it's gonna get," Harry frowned, holding onto the ladder with both hands. "You be careful up there."

"Sure thing, Dad," Tristan quipped snidely but he took the advice.

The top of the wing was slick as hell. Tristan didn't dare try to stand on it. He crawled across until reaching the wing's engine. It wasn't exactly what they had planned but tapping into the system through the engine would work just as well. There would be wires and entire sections that were going to need to be bypassed but it could be done. Popping the panel that gave him access, Tristan left it open as he set up the solar kit. Though lightweight, it was ghastly large when completely unfolded. The thing looked like something you'd see on a satellite in a Sci Fi movie.

Harry was bored out of his mind as Tristan did all the work above him. His eyes scanned the scattered woods surrounding the Z56. This area of Alaska gave the appearance of being utterly desolate. Harry knew it wasn't. There was all kinds of life out there; wolves, bears, deer, rodents, birds. . .God only knew what else. A noise was carried to him on the wind. It was distant and too quiet to make out. Though he couldn't tell exactly what it was, the cries gave Harry fresh chills.

They were drawing closer. Harry tilted his head trying to better make out what the sounds were. Then he could hear them.

"Help!" he heard a man yelling. "We've got wounded here!"

Harry shook his head as if trying to clear it. Who the hell were these people and how did they get here? And how did one of them get wounded? The word choice made his mind spin. Not injured but wounded.

There were three soldiers, two of them dragging along the other between them. They were from the Z56. He couldn't place all their names but Harry knew the hurt one in the middle was Zack. The guy's thick, southern accent left a mark on your memory.

He heard Tristan moving, likely abandoning his work to try and come down the ladder to help.

"Stay where you are!" Harry barked up at Tristan. "I got this!"

Harry left the ladder and ran to meet the trio of soldiers, seeing the large, red soaked bandage over Zack's stomach. The southerner's skin was pale and coated with a sheen of sweat.

"What happened to him?" Harry asked, moving to take the place of the soldier on the left as both of them hauling Zack along were so worn out and haggard it was shocking that they were still able to keep moving like they were.

"Thanks, man." Chad bent over, hands on his knees, catching his breath.

The other was clearly the squad's leader. Harry thought his name might be Weston. And that the other one was named Chad.

"Did he fall or something?" Harry pressed Weston, digging for an explanation to Zack's condition.

"Hell no," Weston growled. "We were attacked out there!"

"We need to get inside right now," Chad said, "All of us and get that door sealed."

"Tristan's up on the wing rigging up some supplemental solar power to stretch out the life of the batteries," Harry glanced from Chad to Weston and back again still trying to make sense of the insanity of it all. Who the hell was out here to attack them? It's not like they'd crash landed into a den of terrorists in the Sandbox.

"Then get him down here!" Weston snapped.

The fear in Weston's eyes spoke volumes. He and the others had been through something horrible. . .something truly horrible. They were shaken up and spooked. Harry knew these guys weren't newbies. They'd seen their shares of blood and death before.

"You heard the man, Tristan!" Harry shouted. "Move it!"

"But I ain't done hooking up. . ." Tristan started to argue.

"I don't give a damn, man!" Weston yelled. "Get down here!"

Realizing, finally, that this wasn't some sick joke and that he might actually be in danger, Tristan left the solar gear behind and crawled towards the ladder as fast as he could. Harry gestured for Weston to take hold of the ladder and hold it steady for him. Weston did but his gaze didn't leave the trees. He was watching for trouble. Chad was too.

Tristan pretty much slid down the ladder, thudding into the icy snow.

Weston lingered, weapon at the ready, as he nodded for everyone else to get into the Z56. When they had, he followed, shoving the heavy metal door behind him.

"Get his thing secured!" Weston snarled at Tristan

Technically, Harry and Tristan weren't part of his unit, much less under his command. The force of Weston's command made Tristan yelp, "Yes sir!" anyway.

****

Colonel Hatch's health was worse. Tony said that likely there were internal injuries that he just didn't have the resources aboard to properly deal with. It wasn't news that Lieutenant Lane wanted to hear. He didn't like being in charge in circumstances like this. Not one damn bit. The crap just kept hitting the fan.

Lieutenant Lane sat on the edge of a bed across the room from where Weston and Chad stood. Mason was in the rest compartment too. Lane wanted him there. The pilot was outside of his command and didn't feel a pressure to agree with whatever he said like many of his men would.

"I've got a gutted soldier in the med bay and this transport sealed up with our engineers terrified to go back outside to finish the work they were doing," Lieutenant Lane said sharply. "Would you gentlemen like to explain to me just how the hell we got to this point?"

Weston had calmed considerably since his return to the Z56. From what he heard, both him and Chad were nearly out of their minds with fear when they first arrived. Chad, from how he was fidgeting, wasn't coping with whatever they ran into out there as well.

"It's simple, sir,"Weston said. "We're not alone."

Lieutenant Lane leaned forward, eyes locked on Weston. "You're going to need to explain that more."

Chad lost it. "There's a fragging monster out there sir! The thing came out of nowhere and ripped Zack open before any of us could do squat. We. . .we shot the crap out of it, sir. We really did but that bastard. . .it wasn't just still standing, the damn thing ran away into the woods."

"Settle down, soldier!" Lieutenant Lane barked.

"Sorry sir," Chad swallowed hard realizing he had gone off at his commanding officer. "I. . ."

"What Chad is trying to say, sir," Weston butted in, taking over, "is the thing we encountered was fast, deadly, and tougher than it had any right to be. Chad's not exaggerating about the amount of fire the thing took though."

"How about you start with telling me just what in the hell the thing was?" Lieutenant Lane prodded him.

"It was a Yeti," Chad said firmly.

Lieutenant Lane had heard the wild rumors that were already circulating since the two of them got back. He hadn't believed them, didn't want to, because if he did that would mean that two of his men had snapped and lost their minds.

"Weston?" Lieutenant Lane's gaze locked onto the calmer man who had been the squad's C.O. while they were out there.

"I don't know what it was, sir," Weston frowned. "Honestly, I don't. I've never seen anything like that creature outside of bad horror movies. It was massive, all muscle and white hair. Violent as hell. That thing wanted us dead. There's no doubt that it's an apex predator in this region but. . .I don't think it wanted to eat us, sir. I think that thing saw us as intruders on its turf and was pissed as hell."

"No chance you killed it?" Lieutenant Lane asked.

Weston shook his head. "We hurt it. The thing was leaving a trail of blood behind when it ran off. I suppose there's a chance that it could have bled out from the damage we did but I doubt it."

Lieutenant Lane grunted. "I see."

"I don't think you do, sir," Weston challenged him. "You've got to be sitting there thinking these two guys are whacko, utterly insane. That's not the case, sir. Whatever that thing is, a Yeti, a Sasquatch, Bigfoot, it's real and it's out there. And as much as I hate to say this, there's no guarantee it's the only one of its kind."

Not really sure of how to respond, Lieutenant Lane just stared at Weston. It was Mason who spoke up to break the silence.

"Primate," Mason interjected. "Let's just call these things primates."

Lieutenant Lane smiled. Having Mason present was paying off as he thought it would. The guy put a name to the unnamable just like that and one that didn't feel as messed up as saying something like Yeti or Bigfoot. The only thing that bothered him was how Mason had instantly latched onto the idea that there was more than one of this beast that attacked his men out there.

"Yes sir," Weston answered., "That's exactly what it was, a primate."

Shifting how he sat to lean back, Lieutenant Lane steepled his fingers in front of his chest, thinking.

"This is a lot to take in and process,"he said. "Did Tony talk like Zack was going to pull through?"

"When I left him, sir," Weston answered, "it was looking pretty bleak."

"Well, gentlemen, primate or not, we have to get this transport repaired and into the air again or at least finish rigging up the solar stuff that Harry and Tristan were on about before all this came up. We can't just sit here sealed up and wait for help to come save our arses. When the backup power goes, we'll all freeze to death and I refuse to let that happen without doing everything I can to prevent it.

"You encountered this primate a good distance from here and claim to have shot the thing to hell," Lieutenant Lane pointed out. "There's no reason to think that it would try to follow you here. From the amount of damage you say you did to it, that thing is likely hiding in a cave somewhere licking its wounds."

"Maybe," Weston said though he hadn't really been asked for his opinion, the lieutenant was just voicing his thoughts aloud.

"Here's what's going to happen," Lieutenant Lane said"First off, you two are going to get some down time. I can't use you in the state that you're in. You two are dismissed. I don't want to see either of you again until you've gotten some rest."

He could see that Weston wanted to argue but was smart enough not to. Lieutenant Lane watched them leave for the other rest compartment then turned to Mason.

"What do you make of all this?" Lieutenant Lane asked the pilot.

Mason appeared shocked to be asked.

"I think that if their story is true, and the evidence at hand certainly supports that it is, we're in some far deeper crap than we already thought,"Mason met his eyes," Only time is gonna tell us just how deep."

Lieutenant Lane's forehead crinkled in thought. "I take it you don't believe that they could have just run into a polar bear that hit them so hard and fast their minds made something of it that it wasn't?"

"Polar bears live in these parts and, yeah, they do attack just about anything that moves when they're hungry," Mason conceded. "But I believe their story. You had to have seen the level of fear in them just like I did. Whatever they ran into, it wasn't any ordinary animal."

"I do too,"Lieutenant Lane admitted. "But what the hell? I mean, you'd think we would catch a break sometime! Crashing and likely being stuck out here wasn't enough, you know? Now we have an honest to God monster running around out there too."

Knuckles rapped against the side of the rest compartment's doorway. Lieutenant Lane and Mason looked to see Tony standing just outside it.

"What now?" Lieutenant Lane threw his hands up in frustration, rather an unseemly thing for an acting commanding officer to do but he was just human.

"Zack is dead," Tony informed them. "I did everything I could for him but he had lost so much blood and my supplies and options here are. . . limited."

"Damn it!" Lieutenant Lane punched the wall next to the bed he sat on. His knuckles met metal. He was lucky not to break anything but the blow still hurt like hell.

"I'm sorry," Tony said, as if taking the blame for everything.

"And the colonel?" Mason asked.

Lieutenant Lane's gaze swiveled around towards him. Did the question indicate that Mason didn't trust his leadership or was his own injured ego beginning to play tricks with his mind? Lane wasn't sure.

"He's getting worse every hour," Tony sighed. "I'm not sure he's going to make it through the night."

"Great," Lieutenant Lane growled.

Tony cocked an eyebrow at him.

"You're dismissed," Lieutenant Lane snapped, the anger in his voice not directed at Tony but enough to put both the medic and Mason on edge. He saw them exchange a concerned glance.

As soon as Tony was gone, Lieutenant Lane got up from his seat and stood there rubbing at the bruised knuckles of his right hand.

"It's a hell of a lot for anyone," Mason commented before he could say anything.

"What's that supposed to mean?" Lieutenant Lane snarled, barely keeping his temper under control.

Mason raised his hands, open palmed, in a gesture of surrender. "I meant being stressed out is understandable. We all are. You're doing a better job at holding everything together than I ever could."

As the pilot's words sunk in, Lieutenant Lane's anger deflated like a balloon. His shoulders slumped in relief. Mason's unexpected approval pulled him back from the edge of snapping.

"Thanks," Lieutenant Lane said.

The lights in the rest compartment flickered.

"Oh fragging hell," Lieutenant Lane rasped.

"We need that emergency solar gear hooked into the Z56's systems a.s.a.p.," Mason got up from where he sat to stand facing him.

"I know," Lieutenant Lane agreed. "I'll assign some guys to go out with Harry and Tristan."

"I'd like to go with them too," Mason said.

Lieutenant Lane didn't argue.

****

"Uh. . ." Tristan shifted nervously on his feet next to the exit door. "You guys sure that we really want to do this?"

Gathered and waiting on him to open the way outside were the three soldiers assigned to protect him and Harry while they worked: Glen, Rich, and

Brewster. Harry was behind them lugging along the tools they were going to need to get things done fast and in one go.

"Tristan! Shut up and get the freaking door open!" Harry yelled.

As Tristan swung the heavy door outward, Glen stepped forward, rifle raised and at the ready, eyes scanning for any lurking threat beyond it. He led the way out, the other soldiers following after him. Tristan held back to fall in behind them with Harry. All of them, himself and Harry included, were wearing night vision goggles.

The world became a crazy shade of bright green as he tugged his into place to cover his eyes. It just made things more creepy than they already were knowing that there could be a real monster out there somewhere. Monsters weren't supposed to exist in the real world. They were the stuff of nightmares, not something tangible and not something that could actually rip your face off. Tristan shuddered, feeling a little sick, as he remembered the amount of blood that leaked out of Zack despite the bandage covering his wound.

"Come on," Harry urged him. "We don't have any time to waste and you damn well know it."

"Right," Tristan said.

Rich and Brewster spread out, searching for any sign of trouble. Glen stuck close to Tristan and

Harry as they got the ladder back into place and secured.

"It'll go faster with both of us up there," Harry told Tristan. "So let's get this done and over with."

Tristan braced the ladder for Harry to go up first. Glen moved in closer to hold it as Tristan followed him up.

From atop the wing they could see the area around the plane a lot better. The scattered woods and snow stretched on towards the horizon in every direction. The solar gear was where he'd left it. The central unit was fixed to the plane's wing and its panels extended. They swayed slightly in the light breeze as Tristan lacked the time earlier to get them all braced as they should be. Getting that done was where he and Harry started. It was the easy part. What came next was wiring the unit directly into the plane's systems and making sure the connection worked. So much of the Z56's wiring was fried. Sure enough, there were several sections that needed bypassing.

As they worked, neither he nor Harry could see the soldiers below the wing who were guarding them. Tristan thought that every once in a while he could hear the frozen snow crunching under their boots. They'd closed the door behind them upon exiting the Z56 so no light spilled out through it. The only light was the stars above but that was more than enough for their night vision goggles to work.

"That should do it," Harry said, getting up from where he worked, wrench in his hand.

An inhuman shriek came from somewhere among the trees to the west. It was unlike anything Tristan had ever heard. The cry was like something out of hell itself. Another answered it from the east.

Eyes bugging, Tristan looked over at Harry. "I thought there was only supposed to be one."

"Stop freaking out," Harry ordered. "We don't know what those noises were."

"Nothing good," Tristan frowned. "You can count on that."

"Let's just get going," Harry said, starting for the top of the ladder.

They had to move carefully because of the icy spots on the wing. One wrong step and they'd be taking one hell of a faceplant, bone against metal, or worse, toppling all the way off to the ground below. That would almost certainly snap a bone or two like twigs.

Harry went first, moving as fast as he could. Tristan was right above him. As Harry leaped from the ladder into the snow, Tristan started down. He was only halfway when all hell broke loose. The shrieking cries rang out in the night again, only now they were much closer and from far more than just two directions.

"Hurry the hell up!" Glen urged Tristan. "Just jump, man!"

Rich and Brewster were no longer spread out and had drawn back closer to the Z56. Harry stood at the bottom of the ladder having taken Glen's place keeping it steady. Both of Glen's hands were now holding his weapon ready.

"Holy mother!" Rich shouted. "Look!"

From all sides of the plane the beasts came, emerging from the trees. There were seven of them in all, at least that could be seen. Their eyes glowed like the interiors of burning furnaces in the squad's night vision view of the world. The shrieks of the creatures fell quiet, replaced by deep rumbling growls as they advanced on the Z56. The things were pretty much as Tristan imagined them. The shortest of them stood over seven feet tall, the largest a hulking nine feet. Their bodies were all powerful muscles and thick, white hair. Gleaming, sharp teeth showed between their snarling black lips.

"Glen!"Brewster called out, clearly wanting him to give the order to open fire.

"Take them down!" Glen barked, taking aim at the closest of the beasts to where he was.

Tristan and Harry didn't need to be told to run like hell for the door leading into the giant transport. They did so as the bullets started flying.

All three of the soldiers' guns were blazing away at the approaching monsters on full auto. Brewster wasn't screwing around, going for the face of the monster he targeted. It recoiled, bringing up its arms to protect the softer flesh there. Bullets pierced flesh beneath long white hair, sending droplets of red flying.

Rich was firing wildly, trying to stop the two powerhouses of primal fury that were charging towards him, their huge feet flinging chunks of frozen snow with each step. His bullets hammered into one then the other as Rich swept his rifle back and forth. Neither of the beasts were even really slowed by the barrage he unleashed upon them.

Rifle chattering on full auto, Glen hosed the beast he engaged. Its snarl grew more furious as bullets tore a swathe of bright red across its chest. The thing picked up its speed, bounding at Glen like a runaway locomotive.

"Holy!" Glen yelped, seeing that his rifle wasn't going to be able to stop the monster before it reached him. He whirled about to run as another beast came from seemingly out of nowhere, plowing into him. The force of the impact lifted Glen from the ground and flung him several yards through the air. He landed, bouncing hard along the snow. Each time he hit jarring him to the bone and bruising him up badly. Glen bit through his tongue on one of them before finally coming to a stop, sprawled out. His mouth filled with the hot wetness of his own blood. He spat out a mouthful of red along with a chunk of his tongue. Glen touched his right side, flinching, sure that several of his ribs were fractured. There was no choice but to fight through the pain. The beast hadn't let up. It was already towering over him. Glen heard its snarl even before he looked up to see it there. A hairy hand came down to clutch Glen by the front of his parka-like arctic gear and the tactical vest beneath it. The beast lifted him effortlessly out of the snow. Glen had managed to hold onto his weapon. Shoving the barrel of his rifle up under the beast's chin, he squeezed the trigger. The rifle barked, spewing rounds. Bullets punctured the soft flesh to tear through the roof of the beast's mouth, traveling on upwards. The move was enough to save Glen's life. Letting go of him, the beast staggered a few steps backwards before collapsing. Glen felt vindicated seeing the blood running freely from its open mouth. The beast's body was twitching in death throes, flailing about on the frozen snow. It warmed his heart too and gave him hope seeing that the big, white haired bastards could die. They weren't unstoppable powerhouses that could just tank all the damage done to them.

Rich's rifle clicked empty before the two charging monsters reached him. He had fired every round into them and yet they didn't even seem fazed by it. There were pockmarks of blood in their white hair but none of the wounds they'd taken were enough to really hurt them. Ejecting the spent magazine, Rich tried to slam a fresh one into place. Before he could, a clawed, hair-covered hand lashed out to knock his rifle from his hands. His trigger finger and the thumb of his right hand went with it. Rich yelped in pain before the beast's other hand shot out for its massive fingers to close around his throat. They tightened, crushing it. Rich's eyes rolled up to show only whites as he struggled and failed to take a final breath. The beast gave a thunderous roar as it flung away his corpse.

Brewster saw Glen go down and Rich die. His brutal onslaught on the beast that had charged him had managed to stop it long enough for him to switch weapons. He'd cast aside his rifle to draw the automatic shotgun from where it was sheathed on his back.

"Rich!" he shouted, running to help his friend even though rationally knowing it was too late. His automatic shotgun boomed in a chain of rapid blasts. Each blew a chunk of bloody meat from the body of the beast that had killed Rich. The beast fell dead, a gory mess of torn flesh. Taking it out had cost Brewster half of his ten round magazine though.

Having avenged Rich, Brewster spun about to see if he could save Glen. The squad leader was hurt but still in the fight having killed a beast of his own. A sudden scream drew Brewster's attention to Harry and Tristan. The two engineers were almost to the door leading inside the Z56. A massive, nine foot tall monster was right on their heels and gaining on them with each long stride of its powerful legs. If he didn't act, they would both be dead in seconds. Brewster's emotions urged him to do what he could for Glen. Logic though dictated that he save Harry and Tristan. Everyone aboard the Z56 needed those two alive.

"Frag it!" Brewster turned his back on Glen and ran to intercept the monster going after Harry and Tristan. Pouring on the speed, he cut directly between it and them, leveling his shotgun at the huge beast's chest. In a thunderous roar Brewster fired off the remainder of his magazine at point blank range. The beast was flung backward as the heavy slugs reduced the front of its upper torso to a mess of splattering, bloody gore.

"Yeah! That's what you get, you shaggy haired mother," Brewster grinned like a maniac.

His moment of victory ended abruptly as a

white, hair-covered hand grabbed him from behind, yanking him up from the snow and flinging him through the air like a child's toy. Brewster landed on his back, air knocked from his lungs. Gasping for breath, he rolled sideways onto his feet, reloading his automatic shotgun as he moved. His vision was blurred by tears as air began to refill his lungs. He heard the monstrous roar of another beast as it came at him from his left flank. Brewster figured he was about to buy the farm but he heard a shouted "get down" at the last possible moment. He threw himself flat on the ground as a cacophony of gunfire erupted from just outside the door leading into the Z56.

Lieutenant Lane himself and two other soldiers had emerged through it and were hammering the beasts with an unexpected barrage of fire that stunned the monsters enough to keep them at bay. Brewster knew that if he wanted to live to see the sun come up, he had to reach the door and get through it to safety. The second the firing slacked, Brewster hurled himself onto his feet and ran like hell for it. He could hear voices calling out, ordering him to move even faster. Legs pumping beneath him and breaths coming as ragged gasps, Brewster reached the entrance as the soldiers there parted to let him through. Then he was inside. From behind him came an explosion. Its shockwave slammed into Brewster, flinging him into the corridor wall. His forehead smacked hard against the metal, vision going white. Brewstar toppled to the floor.

****

Brewster awoke with a start, screaming at the top of his lungs. He sat bolt upright on the medical bed. Tony rushed to place a hand on his chest and shove him back down onto the bed.

"Whoa, buddy!" Tony yelled. "Take it easy! You're safe now!"

Looking around, Brewster realized he was in the Z56's medical bay. His head hurt like hell. His fingers came up to touch his forehead but that only increased the pain to a nearly blinding level.

"Holy hell," Brewster wheezed. "What happened?"

"You nearly got torn apart by those monsters out there," Tony told him. "Don't you remember?"

"I remember killing one of those bastards, maybe more, and then. . . then I'm pretty sure I made it back inside," Brewster half closed his eyes against the pain.

Noticing, Tony frowned. "That bad, huh?"

Brewster managed a weak nod.

"I'm sorry," Tony shook his head. "I can't give you anything for it."

That wasn't what Brewster wanted to hear.

Normally, he didn't care for meds that weren't truly needed but right now. . .he'd take anything if it would make his head stop pounding.

"You're going to have to tough it out," Tony put a hand on his shoulder.

"So did one of those things get me?" Brewster asked. "Is that why I feel like somebody went crazy on my head with a baseball bat?"

"No," Tony said. "You did make it inside. If one of those things had gotten a hold of you, you wouldn't be breathing right now."

"Then what. . .?" Brewster stammered.

"Those things were right behind you, man," Tony explained. "The LT and the others with him were trying to keep them from getting inside too. Markson was carrying some grenades. From how they tell it to me, he stepped forward to throw one and a monster tackled him. You can figure out the rest I'm sure."

"Frag," Brewster muttered.

"Dang right," Tony agreed. "Markson and Clark are both dead."

"What about the LT?" Brewster asked.

"Took some shrapnel in his leg but he made it," Tony answered. "He's limping around likely in as much pain as you are."

"I am guessing those things didn't make it in," Brewster stared at the medic.

"Nope," Tony turned away to fiddle with some medical instruments on a table near where Brewster lay. "Harry and Tristan got the door shut before they could thanks to Markson's grenades going off. I don't know if the blast scared the monsters off or what but none of them even tried to get in after it. Good thing too. As strong as they're supposed to be, who knows if the door would have held or not? The LT has guards posted at it now. . . just in case."

"Damn," Brewster sighed. "What else have I missed?"

"Not much," Tony assured him. "After all that, everything's sort of calmed down a lot. Harry and Tristan succeeded in getting that stuff outside set up before everything went pear shaped. Don't know if you remember that or not. Thanks to that, they say we've gained a good bit more time in terms of the backup power batteries. The LT is pissed though. Everyone's on edge, waiting on those things to come back. Most are worried that if they do, there won't be any stopping them next time."

"And the colonel's still out of it?" Brewster suddenly looked around the medical bay again, eyes searching for him.

Tony grunted. "The colonel's dead, man."

Brewster's eyes bugged. "What?"

Tony nodded grimly. "Internal injuries. Nothing I could do for him here."

The guilt in Tony's voice was thick and heavy.

"You can't blame yourself for that, Tony," Brewster said, even though he knew that Tony wasn't ready to hear what he was saying right now.

Tony ignored what he'd said. "Anyway, a bunch of the guys are wanting to go after those things out there, make sure that they don't come back."

Brewster blinked. He understood what the others had to be feeling but that was insane. Those beasts were like walking tanks and outside of the Z56, they had the home turf advantage too. The beasts knew the lay of the land while they were all strangers to it. Going out there after them even armed to the teeth and knowing what to expect. . . it was still likely suicide.

Tony saw his expression and guessed what he was thinking. He shrugged. "You're free to go, Brewster. I can't keep you here and there's nothing more I can do for you anyway. Just don't push it too hard, okay?"

"No promises on that," Brewster grinned and carefully got up. He was still in uniform but his tactical vest and cold weather parka had been taken off and were laying on the small table at the foot of his bed. Brewster snatched them on his way out.

As he reached the exit, Brewster turned to look back at Tony.

"And thanks, man," he said.

Tony flashed him a wry smirk. "No worries. It is my job to patch you lunkheads up, ya know?"

Brewster headed along the corridor towards the rest compartment the LT had been using as a CIC and briefing room. His gut told him that's where he'd find the LT. Sure enough, as he entered, Brewster saw the LT, Mason, and several others of his unit gathered in it. The LT and Mason were quiet but no one else was. They were all screaming at one another and arguing. The fight was over whether or not to go on the offensive against the monsters or hole up in the Z56 and wait for help to come.

"Enough!" The LT's voice echoed across the rest compartment.

Everyone fell silent instantly.

"We've lost five people to those monsters out there already, "the LT snapped. "I'm not inclined to lose any more."

"We can't just wait here though," Mason unexpectedly chimed in.

"That dude's right!" Lucas belted out. "If we sit here and do nothing, they'll come for us!"

"Yeah," Han backed him up. "If those things really want to get in here, I don't think we can stop them. Not if even half of what I've heard about them are true."

"It's all true," Brewster said, joining the conversation.

"Brewster," the LT recognized him. "Glad to see you up and about."

"Thank you, sir," Brewster responded.

Brewster looked at the bandage around Lieutenant Lane's right leg. It was just above his right knee. The barest hint of red was seeping through it. Lieutenant Lane was appraising him as well.

"I have seen those things out there up close and personal too, Brewster," Lieutenant Lane said, breaking the moment of silence. "I know how damn tough and fast they are, dangerous sons of. . ."

"Then you know that Mason is right, sir," Brewster frowned. "That door is tough but if enough of those things put their muscles together, it's coming off its hinges and they'll be in this plane with us."

"A fight in here would be just as bad as us trying to go after them out there" Sergeant Hall joined the conversation, saying, "Tristan and Harry have made sure there are no fuel leaks or anything else that could cause this plane to blow but one bullet in the wrong place, one grenade tossed out of desperation in the wrong section. . ." the pilot let his words trail off.

Lieutenant Lane flung his hands up in disgust. "So we can't go after them and we can't stay here either! Just what in the hell is it you're suggesting we do, Mason? Or am I misunderstanding you that you're against both?"

"I am saying we need to think outside the box," Mason smirked. "The best defense is a good offense. . . and we have the means to go on one hell of an offensive if you're willing."

"No," Lieutenant Lane realized what the pilot was getting at. "You can't be serious."

"The suits," Sergeant Hall sucked in an astonished breath.

"Hell yeah," Brewster smiled.

"The X2s have never been fully tested," Lieutenant Lane pointed out. "That's why we're up here in the first place. We were taking them so they could go through a full shakedown."

"All the more reason to give them a go," Mason chuckled. "It's not like we have anything to lose by trying at this point."

"Those suits are worth a fortune, not to mention highly classified and extremely important to some very powerful folks," Lieutenant Lane continued to play devil's advocate. "If we use them and manage to survive this crap, we could all be facing court martials when we get home."

"Better court martial than dead," Mason shrugged.

"I think using them is the only option we've got that makes any sort of sense, sir," Sergeant Hall said.

Brewster had always been impressed by Sergeant Hall. She was the living example of a level headed and fair commanding officer. It didn't hurt that she was attractive either. Maybe it was wrong to think that but she was. Shelby, he never called her that out loud, had pale skin in sharp contrast to her midnight black hair. It was tied in a tight knot behind her head. Her body was slim and sleek, muscles tight. Sometimes Brewster wished he could just stare into her bright green eyes. He could lose himself there for an eternity. Brewster knew he could. But that was never going to happen. She was too by the book and he was too. . . erratic. At least that was what a lot of his commanding officers over the years called him. If he didn't always manage to get the job done, Brewster figured he'd have been booted out of the military all together long ago. Instead, he'd just never advanced in rank as most with his level of skills would have. It was clear to Brewster that those of higher rank saw him as a useful tool though one that sometimes needed to be monitored closely.

The colonel hadn't been any different. That really didn't bother Brewster. Being in the military gave him a purpose and direction he would never have found outside of it. Still, staring at Shelby, glimpses of another kind of life danced through his head. His heart skipped a beat as he caught himself and woke up as if from a dream, hoping no one had noticed how his eyes had been locked onto Shelby with such longing passion.

"Brewster," Lieutenant Lane asked, voice cold and annoyed. "Did you have something you wanted to add?"

Mind racing, not knowing exactly what or how much he'd missed while zoned out, he snapped, "No sir!"

That got a chuckle out of the lieutenant. Sergeant Hall looked at him as if trying to figure out why he was suddenly so seemingly lost and on edge. Mason just sat where he was, a smirk on his lips.

Lieutenant Lane looked to Sergeant Hall and Mason. "If we do this, if we can even get the suits powered up, do any of us know how to use the things?"

Sergeant Hall took them all by surprise. "I do."

"You want to explain that, Sergeant?" Lieutenant Lane urged.

"I put in for a transfer to the Mecha Corps a

while back, went through their version of Basic but didn't make the cut," Sergeant Shelby was clearly down about that.

"I see," Lieutenant Lane nodded slowly, not pressing the issue of why she hadn't.

"I had issues with the neural interface," Sergeant Hall admitted on her own. "They booted me for medical reasons."

"Good to know, Sergeant," Lieutenant Lane appeared to be both relieved and stressed simultaneously. "That means you know how to run the suits then?"

"One hundred percent, sir," Sergeant Hall confirmed.

"I take it that means that you can get those things fired up then?" Lieutenant Lane asked.

"Of course," Sergeant Hall shot a glance at Mason. "I can teach whoever you want me to how to use them as well. I'll just go ahead and say Mason is likely the best candidate here to pilot one of the other suits. His skill set makes him perfect for them. As to who can run the other four, you pick 'em and I'll see if they can handle it."

"Whoa," Mason held up a hand, "I don't know if that's a good idea!"

"I realize you're not Army, Mason, and as thus technically outside of my command but given the circumstances. . ." Lieutenant Lane was scowling.

"There's a hell of a lot of difference between a fighter and a mech suit," Mason argued.

"It's not so much about the controls," Sergeant Hall cut in. "It's about piloting instincts and you have them."

"I can't order you to do this, Mason," Lieutenant Lane frowned. "I believe that Sergeant Hall is right about you though. We all need you to get in one of those suits if we're going to go through with this plan."

Reluctantly, Mason gave in. "I get that. I'll give it a go and we'll see."

"We'll still need four more pilots," Sergeant Hall said.

"I want to try," Brewster spoke up instantly.

Sergeant Hall, Shelby, turned to give him an appraising look. Apparently he had surprised her as much as he had everyone else just moments before.

"Mason, Brewster, you're in then. Obviously I can't," the LT patted his injured leg. "I'll have the others report to you in pairs. Put them through the motions and see what you think. I trust your judgement, Sergeant."

The LT didn't say that he really didn't have a choice in that. Of all of them, only Shelby had ever been in one of the suits before.

****

The bay where the X2 suits were kept was lit only by dim, red emergency lighting. The Z56's automatic systems cut the bulk of the power to it aside from that directed into the cocoon-like stations where the X2s were strapped in and stored. Tristan manually turned up the lights as he, Shelby, Mason, and Brewster entered. No one had asked him about trying out to pilot a suit but Tristan had volunteered as they had met up with him on the way to the bay. Shelby hadn't turned him down. If the tech worked out as a pilot, that left only lacking two more to man all of the X2s for the offensive that lay ahead.

Shelby stepped right up to the master controls for the storage units of the X2s and keyed in the code to open them fully up. As they were, the suits sat only partially exposed. The pieces of metal holding them in place slid back revealing them. . . the suit directly in front of her opened up. Its chest and upper legs parted to reveal a compartment for the suit's pilot to climb into.

"Okay guys," Shelby said getting everyone's attention. "Here are some of the basics you're going to need to know. These bad boys are called X2s. They're powered by mini-fusion reactors. Fusion not fission. That means a meltdown is impossible even if they get damaged in combat."

Sergeant Shelby Hall walked up to the suit next to the one that had opened up, rapping her knuckles against its metal. "The X2s are heavily armored. Small arms fire is pretty much useless against them barring an extremely lucky shot or something firing .50 cal rounds at you."

Moving over to the open suit, Shelby gestured at its innards. "As you can see, this is the pilot compartment. Once you're sealed up inside, you will have your own sealed environment with enough air for eight hours. That said, the suit can use atmospheric air as well if you don't want to or need to rely on its systems. Now, the X2, while you're in it, is going to enhance your strength by a factor of ten. You'll be able to do the superhero thing and punch through walls, rip apart cars, and lift an incredible amount of weight. And the legs of these things are no less than the arms. They'll give you increased jumping power. You won't be able to fly but you might feel like you are in some circumstances."

"What about firepower?" Brewster asked.

Sergeant Hall grinned from ear to ear. "Oh yeah, they've got enough to take on just about anything on the ground that could possibly come at them. Each X2 has a choice of primary weapons that they carry, those being a backpack, belt fed, tri-barrel .50 caliber or a multipurpose, M82

Barrett rifle variant. That variant uses one hundred, .50 caliber magazines, but also is equipped with a grenade launcher beneath the primary barrel with up to eight rounds of its own. The rifle uses the Barrett's original sights and is accurate from equal distances but is also able to be switched to both burst and fully automatic fire for close range engagements. There's also an automatic, combat shotgun available for the X2s. Each has a 50 round magazine. Thankfully the X2s are built to completely absorb the recoil of such a weapon. You won't even feel the kick."

"Damn," Brewster was impressed.

"That's not all though," Sergeant Hall continued with a gleam in her eyes. "The X2s come equipped with internal secondary weapons. Within each arm are mini-rocket launchers, the left anti-armor and the right fragmenting anti-personnel. But that's not all, folks. The right arm also has an extendable combat blade."

"No way," Mason said in disbelief.

"Yep," Sergeant Hall assured him. "An honest to God, freaking sword, with all the X2's strength behind each swing. And the left arm has a top mounted, internally fed, machine gun loaded with a hundred rounds. Less than .50 caliber but still packing a good punch."

Mason was shaking his head. "Jeez. These

things are insane."

"Yes they are," Sergeant Hall said with pride. "That's why I signed up to be an X2 pilot. So who wants to try one on first?" Sergeant Hall asked.

Brewster and Mason exchanged a glance. Tristan looked excited and terrified at the same time.

"After you, sir," Brewster motioned for the pilot to go first.

"Tristan?" Mason offered.

"No thanks, man," Tristan took a step back away from the suits. "I'm happy with going last."

Brewster slapped the tech on the back. "Hey, don't worry. We're glad you're here trying."

"Alright then, sir, it looks like you're up," Sergeant Hall motioned Mason forward. "When the suit closes over you, you're going to feel a connection made to the rear of your neck. Don't panic over it and don't fight it. It'll be the neural interface that ties you into the X2s' systems. It won't hurt but it will feel odd. I'm not sure I can explain it in words. Just trust me that it's normal."

"Sure," Mason reluctantly climbed up and into the X2 in front of him. The armor sealed itself over him. He felt the connection he'd been warned about getting made then. . . he saw the world very differently. It felt differently too. The bulletproof glass of the suit's faceplate lit up with a tactical display and he knew from the interface that he could adjust his vision in terms of its range and darkness functionality level. He mentally flexed his hand and the suit's was what made the motion not his flesh and blood one. His entire body was held, tight and locked in place. It was strange controlling everything with only his thoughts but that was how the X2 worked.

Sergeant Hall gave him an excited thumbs up. "You're doing great. Now I want you to very slowly walk forward. Just think about putting one foot in front of the other and do it."

Mason sucked in a breath, steeling himself, and followed her instructions. The suit lurched out of its storage compartment. Its first few steps were awkward and wobbly but each step Mason had the X2 take, the more comfortable he became at controlling it.

"Good!" Sergeant Hall yelled excitedly. "You're doing great."

The right hand of Mason's X2 returned her earlier thumbs up and then moved to stand across from where the other X2s sat.

Sergeant Hall helped Brewster and Tristan into their own X2s next. Brewster handled his worse than Mason had. His X2 dropped onto its left knee as he tried to walk it out of its storage area. With Sergeant Hall encouraging him, Brewster righted the mech and got it to stand up, finally moving to join Mason on the other side of the compartment.

Shockingly, Tristan took to his X2 like a fish to water. The movements of his suit were smooth and graceful as the mech emerged and crossed the room.

"Wow," Sergeant Hall remarked, praising him, "And you were worried."

"Still am," Tristan's voice came through the armor's exterior speaker. "Walking and heading into combat are two entirely different things."

"That suit is tougher than a tank, Tristan," Sergeant Hall assured him. "You're going to be just fine."

As Sergeant Hall stood looking at her three trainees, three more soldiers entered the compartment - Samuel, Paul, and Dave. Sergeant Hall was surprised to see Dave. He wasn't someone that she would have thought the LT would have chosen to pilot an X2. At least he'd never struck her that way. Dave was a very quiet guy and seemed very down to earth and by the book, ever cautious. Not exactly the sort you'd want in a prototype war machine. He was thin with sharp facial features. Often, Sergeant Hall thought Dave was a hell of a lot smarter than his appearance and mannerisms suggested. Samuel on the other hand was the epitome of a grunt. It was a mystery to her how Samuel had even made it into special forces. Paul was just your average trooper. Nothing stood out about him to Sergeant Hall, either good or bad.

Brewster, Mason, and Tristan waited patiently while Sergeant Hall got the three of them into their suits and ran through getting them to walk across the room. She then had all six of them try out some basic motions. Sergeant Hall wasn't about to let any of them try out the X2s' weapon systems inside the Z56.

"Okay fellows," Sergeant Hall said, "We've done all we can do in here. We're gonna have to take this outside."

"Outside?" Tristan croaked.

"I trust you all can walk down the rear cargo ramp without embarrassing me?" Sergeant Hall asked.

"Yes ma'am," her students chorused back at her.

****

Lieutenant Lane had cleared them to open up the rear cargo door long enough for the squad of X2s and Sergeant Hall to leave the transport. The feet of the mechs clanged loudly as they walked down the ramp into the snow. As soon as they were all out, it rose, closing up in their wake. Sergeant Hall looked horridly out of place standing with the huge, armored mechs in just cold weather gear.

The hood of her parka was pulled up to protect her ears from the chill of the wind and she wore a cloth over the lower half of her face. Sergeant Hall's eyes were protected too by goggles.

The sun was beginning to rise, bright first rays cutting through the dark. There was no sign of the monsters other than their tracks and the damage they had done to the exit door below the pilot compartment. Its metal was dented and paint was scraped away by claws.

"Damn," Brewster commented. "Those bastards must be strong as hell."

"You can bet safely on that," Tristan blurted out.

Ignoring their banter, the head of Mason's X2 craned downward to observe Sergeant Hall.

"Sergeant," Mason said, "Are you sure you shouldn't be in one of these mechs?"

Mason saw that his question pained her.

Frowning, Sergeant Hall answered, "I wish. Can't though. Every time I get in one I risk completely burning out my nervous system or so the docs tell me."

"I can imagine what that has to be like," Mason told her.

"Can you now?" She asked, voice filled with sincere doubt.

"If I could never fly again," Mason said, "I might just shoot myself."

Sergeant Hall chuckled at that.

"Maybe you do get it," she admitted. "But we've got to get focused here. All of you, I want you to turn southward, activate your combat systems and pick a target."

It only took a single thought for Mason to shift the X2 he was in to full combat mode. His senses felt keener. He focused on the tactical data that was both before his eyes on the interior of the suit's faceplate and being fed directly into his mind as well.

Targeting was far easier than he thought it would be. It looked to be that way for the others too. Sergeant Hall talked them through firing off a few rounds and getting a feel for the combat functions of the suits. There was no danger of the X2s running out of power. Mason, like some of the others likely, had misunderstood that it wasn't a fear of that which kept the lieutenant from using the suits to set out for the base they had been headed to but rather the fact that there were only six suits. Using them for such a purpose would have left everyone else aboard the Z56 still alone with no communications. Mason was sure that the lieutenant was happy that he hadn't used them to send for help at the base now because those left would have been at the mercy of the giant beasts.

When Sergeant Hall felt like she had put them

all through the proper paces, she ordered them back inside knowing that the newbies at least were competent enough not to get themselves killed. Lieutenant Lane was waiting for them in the main cargo bay in the rear of the Z56. Sergeant Hall moved to stand behind as those in the X2s filed out into an ordered line facing them. Sergeant Hall leaned over whispering something to the lieutenant. He smiled.

"No need to get out of those suits, gentlemen," Lieutenant Lane told them. "Sergeant Hall assures me that you're as ready as we can make you with the time at hand. As thus, you need to head right on out and start your hunt. Sergeant Hall has shown you how to use your suits to locate the Z56 should you be unable to find your way back on your own. You'll be splitting up into three pairs - Brewster and Tristan, Mason and Samuel, Dave and Paul. Brewster, you guys will head north. Mason, you guys get west, and Dave, your squad will head east. I want those damn things out there found and blown to bits. Do you understand me?"

"Yes sir," Everyone but Mason chorused back, even Tristan. Mason didn't, not because he didn't understand but because he didn't feel like it. He was outside of the lieutenant's command and had bowed to Lane enough already. Mason didn't dislike the lieutenant or have anything against him, he just wanted to remind Lane of that fact.

"Good hunting!" Sergeant Hall called to them all as they turned to head out.

Mason not only understood the logic of what they were doing, he'd championed the idea of it. Now though, inside an X2 himself, he was questioning that choice. The suit's systems were surprisingly easy to get used to. And the things really did pack an arsenal of firepower. Rationally, going out to hunt the beasts down before they stormed the Z56 and ended the lives of everyone aboard it made sense. There was a feeling of unease that Mason just couldn't shake though.

The rear door of the Z56 opened once again to let them back out into the cold. Mason and Samuel led the way, the other X2s following in their wake. There was a loud clang as the cargo bay closed up, sealing the huge transport against the dangers outside of it.

The heavily armored mechs split up, each pair marching away from the Z56 in the directions they were assigned. Mason and Samuel moved away from the sun where it had risen in the sky. The snow glared brightly in its growing light. It was still before noon. The stress and lack of sleep was beginning to catch up to Mason. That feeling triggered the X2's internal systems. Mason sucked in a startled breath as he felt a prick in his right arm. Then suddenly he was fully awake and almost superhumanly alert. The suit had shot him up with a powerful stimulant.

"What the hell?" Mason wondered aloud.

All the X2s had their exterior speakers switched off now and were communicating through closed circuit comm. channels. Samuel heard him over it.

"Something wrong?" Samuel asked.

"I accidently shot myself up with stims," Mason admitted. "Be careful what you're thinking. It's like these things can read your mind. One wrong thought and who knows what could happen?"

Samuel laughed.

Mason wasn't joking but it was obvious Samuel was taking what he had said as if he was.

"Nice of those things to leave us tracks to follow," Samuel said, changing the subject.

And it was true. The great beasts' tracks had been everywhere around the Z56. It was easy to follow them. The prints were deep and easy to see as the snow that was just barely beginning to fall again had yet to cover them.

"Yeah, I guess so," Mason answered as if his mind were on auto-pilot, following through the motions of their conversation as his focus was elsewhere. The X2s all stood eight feet in height. Though they appeared bulky their movements were smooth and agile. Mason's eyes were fixed on the tracks in the snow. The head of his suit tilted downward.

"Crazy, ain't it?" Samuel chuckled again.

"Huh?" Mason looked up. He could imagine the wry grin that was likely on Samuel's face within his own X2. "What do you mean?"

"Take a look at us," Samuel clanged one of his X2's fists into the armor plating of his suit's chest. "We're out here in freaking mech suits, marching through a frozen wasteland, hunting monsters, man! Ain't nothing sane about any of that. If you'd told me we'd be doing this yesterday, I would have laughed until I cried and thought you were full of crap. I mean, come on, it's like we booted reality out the window and replaced it with. . . with a cheesy Sci Fi flick or something."

Mason couldn't argue any of that. Every word Samuel just said was true. It made Mason think of a pulp horror novel he'd read a few years ago. The book took place on an alien world where colonial marines found themselves locked in a battle for survival with a world full of monstrous, primate-like creatures. The thing he remembered the most about it was how the author hadn't skimped on the level of gore within its pages.

"Well, let's hope things end better for us than they usually do in those films," Mason commented.

The two of them marched on in silence for a

while. The Z56 had been left far behind them. Though the interior of his X2 was warm and comfortable, Mason could still almost feel the cold seeping into his bones. The world around them was all leafless trees and frozen snow. Fresh snow, flurries maybe, floated about on the light wind. The X2s not only moved smoother than one would expect but they were quieter too, not silent by any means, but there were no clanging sounds of metal like if they were wearing old school plate mail or were robots out of a black and white TV show.

The tracks of the beasts had led them up into some small hills. The trees were denser and they had to pick their path more cautiously to make their way through them. They didn't want to get separated, lose the trail of the beasts, or give up too much of their visibility. The farther away they could see the beasts coming from, the better off they would be.

Samuel was on point, Mason's X2 trailing a dozen yards behind his. The sudden move caught Mason off-guard. His head swept around, eyes searching for any sign of whatever it was that Samuel must have spotted.

"What's up?" Mason asked over their shared commlink.

"We're not alone," Samuel answered.

Mason looked about again but still didn't see

crap. Everything was as calm and quiet as it had been since they'd left the Z56.

"These things, man. . ." Samuel whispered despite not needing to. The creatures had no means of listening in on the comm channel they were using. "They're really starting to creep me out. My X2's systems tell me they're all around us but I don't see any sign of them."

"I don't either," Mason responded, realizing that his own X2 had been trying to tell him exactly what Samuel had. Maybe that was where the feeling of dread he'd been being consumed by was coming from. There were no active targets on his tactical display but there was conflicting data coming from the A.I. suggesting that the beasts were extremely close to their location, if not right on top of them.

Mason wasn't a combat soldier. He was a pilot. . .and more than a bit freaked out.

"What do we. . ." Mason started to ask but never got to.

A hulking, white monster, snarling with primal rage, flung itself from behind the thick, wide trunk of a tree at Samuel. The beast slammed into his X2 like a runaway train, knocking Samuel off balance. His X2 toppled into the frozen snow with the monster atop it. Massive, hair-covered hands pounded the armor of Samuel's suit, leaving smears of blood from torn knuckles and dents on it. Mason blinked. Dents. The thing's blows were actually damaging the X2's armor. He didn't dare open fire on the monster. With the beast right on top of Samuel it couldn't be done without hitting him too. Maybe a better, more experienced X2 pilot might have managed it, Mason was sure he couldn't.

Samuel fought back furiously. The hands of his X2 caught the beast's arms by their wrists. It was like watching a demented wrestling match as the brute force of nature and advanced technology faced off against each other. The servo motors in Samuel's X2 were straining to their limits. If it had been just a man or even a bear that was atop Samuel, its arms would have been ripped bloodily from their sockets. . . but the beast was as strong as the X2, if not a hair stronger.

Mason's attention was drawn away from Samuel's struggle as several more of the creatures emerged from the woods. They were all of various sizes ranging from seven feet in height to nine feet. The largest of them threw its head back in a thunderous roar as the others sprang forward.

Having opted to carry the belt fed .50 caliber tri-barrel, Mason opened fire with the massive weapon. The monsters in the lead of those on the way to him were cut to shreds by the stream of high powered rounds that poured into them. One had its guts ripped wide in an explosion of blood and gore. Ruptured snakes of intestines flew out like popping firecrackers as bullets continued to punch through them. Another of the beasts took a blast to its groin. The thing gave a shrieking yelp, grabbing at what was left of the mess the bullets made between its legs before slumping forward into the snow onto its knees. The entire area of its groin and the hands now clutching it were slicked a bright red. Mason arced the barrel of the tri-barrel upwards at a slight angle as its stream of bullets cut a swathe of mangled meat from one of the beast's groin to the lower part of its neck. That beast died instantly, flung over, to land on its back, body twitching in its death throes. The remaining beasts who had emerged from the trees turned to flee. Mason, determined to keep the momentum he'd gained in the battle, kept right on firing at them. Bullets drilled a hole into the back of a retreating beast before exploding out the front of its chest. A series of rapid clicks came from his weapon followed by a high pitched whine as its barrels spun without any ammo flowing through them. Mason realized what had happened and flung the empty weapon aside.

The snarling face of the beast he fought with peered down at Samuel with eyes that seemed to glow in the light of day. Saliva dripped onto the faceplate of his armor. He looked up to meet the gaze of pure primal rage and fury. Desperate, his X2's rifle lost when the beast tackled him, Samuel maneuvered his right hand to get it under the beast's chin. With a loud thunking noise, his suit deployed its combat blade. The super dense alloy arm-sword plunged into and through the beast's skull, entering through softer flesh, the tip bursting through bone atop the beast's head. Samuel rolled the hairy corpse away and his X2 lumbered up onto its feet.

"Hey!" He shouted over the comm.

Mason wasn't paying attention to him though. He was focused on the monsters. The hulking, nine foot tall bastard that appeared to be the leader of at least those that were present in the attack on them, stood its ground as those retreating ran by it. Raising his left arm, Mason used the suit's tactical system to lock onto the monster. Blazing a burning streak through the frigid air, the rocket launched from his X2 struck the huge monster dead on. The beast's body flew apart into bits of cooked meat and sizzling globs of fatty tissue. By then, Samuel had managed to reach Mason's side.

"Mason," Samuel rasped.

The pilot turned his X2's head to look at the soldier. Mason's blood was boiling inside his veins.

He was blinded by anger and fear-based tunnel vision. His only thoughts were those of destroying the creatures that had escaped into the woods. He couldn't even form the words to respond to Samuel. X2 lunging forward, Mason moved to go after them.

Samuel reached out, grabbing him. "Hold the hell up, man!"

Mason didn't. Breaking free of Samuel's grasp, the legs of his X2 pumped like pistons. He had reached the woods and was within them in only seconds. He plowed straight through several trees, smashing them into showers of raining splinters. He skidded to a halt, panting inside his armor. Sweat slicked his skin and drenched his hair. Mason shook his head as much as was possible inside the X2, trying to clear it. Slowly, he came to his senses. . . but it was too late. He'd given away his advantage and left himself open on all sides. Mason didn't see the beast coming for him until the small tree trunk it swung like a baseball bat crashed into his left shoulder. The trunk was shattered against the metal it met but hit Mason's suit with enough force to send him reeling. Before Mason could recover another beast came from seemingly nowhere. A hair-covered, clenched fist slammed into the abdomen of Mason's X2. Like a human, the heavy armor folded forward in reaction to the blow. Caught so utterly unready for an attack, it was difficult for Mason to regain his balance, both with the armor and mentally. Thankfully, Samuel showed up to save him.

A voice howled a war cry over the commlink between the two X2s as Samuel came running up, flinging himself into the battle. Why the hell Samuel hadn't bothered to recover his rifle was beyond Mason's understanding. Samuel engaged the pair of beasts with his suit's sword. The metal of its already gore-smeared blade swiped through the air leaving a long, deep gash across the chest of the beast that had just struck Mason. Yelping like an injured dog, the beast backed off. The other beast was still clutching the remains of the tree trunk it had used as a bat. It charged forward, using the jagged, broken end like some sort of deranged spear. Samuel attempted to knock its end aside with his sword but failed. The blade merely cut away a chunk of the wood as the beast came barreling on, slamming the trunk into him. The beast's brute strength was enough to send Samuel's X2 staggering sideways. Pressing in, the beast dropped the even more splintered tree trunk and switched tactics. Sparks flew as the claws of its right hand tried to slash Samuel's armor, scratching up along the side of its head. Samuel countered, lashing out with his sword, hoping to drive the beast away from him if only for a second. The beast leaped back out of the blade's reach. Samuel staggered, finding his balance. He and the beast stood facing one another. It snarled at him showing rows of yellow, razored teeth.

"Come on, you mother," Samuel raged. "Bring it on."

The beast responded by doing just that, lunging forward to land a vicious uppercut that nearly ripped the head of his X2 from its armored shoulders and his along with it. The blow left Samuel stunned. He swung about wildly again with his sword. Its swipes through the air were so wild and erratic that the agile monster easily avoided them. Samuel just couldn't catch a break. His vision was blurred inside the X2 and his ears ringing. Watering eyes blinking rapidly, Samuel cried out, raging against his luck and refusing to accept the death that appeared to be coming for him. The beast swung a hair-covered fist and this time Samuel met it at the wrist with his sword. In a spray of bright red, the fist was severed from the arm it was attached to. The fist spun, flinging drops of blood as it went to land in the snow several yards away. The beast gave a grunt of pain. Samuel thrust his blade forward like a professional fencer aiming for the center of the beast's chest. Its other hand caught the blade to stop it. The move stopped the blade from sinking into its heart but as Samuel jerked it out of the beast's grasp, half of its hand was cut away leaving only a bloody mess and a thumb. Eyes going wide in shock, the beast held up what was left of his hand before its face, watching the blood spurt out as Samuel struck his finishing blow. He stepped forward to the side of the beast bringing the blade of his X2's sword full force into the thick muscle of the white, hair-covered neck. The blade thudded into it unable to cut all the way through. Even so, it severed the massive artery beneath the skin there. Blood flowed in rivers down the beast's body and sprayed out around the blade, crescendoing an explosion of wet red as Samuel wrenched the sword free. Slumbering forward onto its knees the beast swayed for a moment and then collapsed, face down, into the snow.

Mason's unexpected arrival had evened the odds of the battle and bought him the time to recover. Launching himself against the beast that had gut punched him, Samuel had bloodied the monster. The wound wasn't deep or mortal but it had given the beast pause. Mason didn't pop his own arm sword. Instead he engaged the beast hand to hand delivering a punch to the side of its face that caused teeth and blood to go flying. The blow was so powerful that the beast couldn't recover before

Mason closed. He paid the bastard back for the unexpected gut punch he had taken, pummeling it with a barrage of rapid fire jabs like a professional boxer. Metal met nature, over and over, each strike bruising and ripping flesh and crunching bone. The beast's face looked like pulped meat as Mason finally withdrew. Somehow the creature was still standing. Mason popped his right arm, mini machine gun, firing point blank. Though the rounds weren't .50 caliber they blasted completely through the beast's head ,exiting the rear of its skull, leaving gaping exit wounds in their wake. There was a loud thud as the beast's corpse toppled over to the ground.

Mason hurried to help Samuel only to see that the beast he'd been fighting was dead too. Samuel had won his battle but his X2 was more than just dinged up. There were dents in the armor and grooves up one side of its head left by what had to have been the claws of the beast Samuel had fought. Mason wondered if his own X2 looked as rough. Regardless, the battle was over. There were no signs of any beasts close by to them.

Samuel came marching determinedly towards him.

"Damn you, Mason!" The soldier spat. "What the hell were you thinking running off like that? You nearly got us both killed, man!"

Mason raised the hands of his X2, open palmed, in a gesture of surrender, trying to get Samuel to calm down.

"Sorry," Mason stammered, "I'm sorry. I lost it, okay? You have to remember I'm not used to this crap like you are!"

"I should beat the holy living crap out of you, Mason," Samuel huffed.

"It won't happen again," Mason promised.

Samuel sucked in a breath so loudly that Mason heard it over the comm.

"So. . .what now?" Mason asked. "Do we keep hunting or head back?"

"Damned if I know if that's a good idea or not," the armored shoulders of Samuel's X2 shrugged. "But. . .orders are orders, Mason. So yeah, we go on."

****

Dave and Paul were packing some heavy fire power. Both of their X2s were carrying belt fed, .50 caliber tri-barrels. They were eager to dish out some payback to the beasts out here. . . if they could find them. Neither of them were truly experienced trackers. They were relying mostly on the hopes that the beasts were going to find them. It was a solid plan. If the things had attacked the Z56 for crashing in their turf then it just made sense for them to want to eliminate all the intruders on it.

Paul's teeth chewed at the left side of his jaw, nipping at the flesh there. It was a bad habit Paul fell into after giving up smoking. Sometimes he really messed up his cheek, others it wasn't so bad. Paul liked to tell himself that regardless it was preferable to smoking. He didn't want to die wheezing and coughing like his father had two years earlier.

"Where the hell are they?" Paul snorted, frustrated and ticked off at their inability to find a single one of the beasts so far.

"Don't worry," Dave said, "They're coming, buddy. You can count on that."

"How the hell do you know that?" Paul griped.

"How can you not?" Dave chuckled. "With our luck, we'll run into the motherload of those things."

"Promises, promises," Paul lightened up, smirking.

Their two X2s marched up a small hill, side by side, though with several yards between them. The trees were spread out in this section of the woods. There still wasn't anything to see but snow and leafless branches. The sun was high in the sky now and blazing down. Its rays lit up the bits of ice in the snow making them glitter and gleam. Paul was almost tempted to use his X2's vision adjustments to darken it all. He might have too except for the tracks they were following. As creepy as the imprints in the snow were, Paul couldn't get enough of them. There were numerous creatures from what he could tell. He counted at least six different pairs of feet among the tracks.

"Will you stop staring so long at those prints," Dave urged.

"What else is there to do right now?" Paul sighed.

"Daydream about being in the city with our girlfriends and eating Kimbap?" Dave quipped.

As they trudged down the other side of the hill, descending into the slight valley below, neither Paul nor Dave was ready for what was waiting for them. All but one set of footprints abruptly ended.

Paul glanced in Dave's direction. He'd noticed too. There was just no explaining it. It was as if the beasts they were following just vanished into thin air or rather all but one of them had.

They reached the bottom of the hill and continued on. The trees up ahead were going to be more closely packed and denser once they were through the open area between the hill and the woods. Paul and Dave walked on. Dave was pulling slightly ahead as all hell broke loose. Up from beneath the snow the beasts sprang out in ambush.

A pair of impossibly strong, clawed hands grabbed the legs of Dave's X2 and yanked them out from under him. Dave's X2 crashed to the ground. His tri-barrel fired, barrels spinning, and a stream of .50 caliber rounds spraying about wildly. His desperate blast caught a beast, shredding its guts and splattering bits of them everywhere. The beast that had laid him low though escaped being hit. Pulling itself closer, the thing snatched at the belt feeding Dave's tri-barrel. The belt snapped. Dave's gun ran empty using up the final rounds available to it then erupted into a high pitched whine until he released its trigger. Dave rolled, refusing to give the beast on him a chance to go after his X2's faceplate. The blow that fell on him clanged against the suit's armored shoulder instead, denting it. The impact jarred Dave roughly inside the X2. He shot an elbow backwards. It crunched into the beast's nose with a sickening crunching noise. That was enough to buy Dave a chance to bring his upper body around so that he could bring the mini-machine gun on his suit's right arm to bear. It chattered, spitting bullets. They raked over the beast from its sternum to the end of its left shoulder, cutting a bloody mangled swathe, turning white hair a wet red. Roaring more in fury than pain, the beast grabbed his arm. The machine gun bent from the pressure of its grip, the round in it blowing. It was Dave's turn to scream as his own right hand was pulped from the small explosion and his suit opened up to the cold air outside of its sealed and heated environment. Dave tried to lurch his suit up onto its feet but another beast appeared above him. A huge foot was rammed downward into the chest of his X2, slamming him back to the ground.

Paul wasn't faring any better. The pair of beasts that sprang up to try to bring him to the ground using the same tactic as the one that succeeded in taking Dave down failed. As they burst from beneath the snow, Paul jumped forward, getting clear of their grasping hands. He spun around hosing them with fire from his tri-barrel. The bodies of the beasts twitched and spasmed as .50 caliber rounds tore apart their torsos in eruptions of blood and gore. Eyeballs burst, lips were torn loose to flop below shattering teeth, and ribs snapped as bullets broke them. Paul whooped in victory then turned to try to help Dave. That was his mistake. He hadn't seen the other beasts off to the sides of those he'd massacred. They rushed him together. One came up directly from behind, its arms slipping through his own, locking him into a wrestling-style hold and causing Paul's tri-barrel to slip from his X2's hands. The beast held him roughly. The servo motors of Paul's X2 strained and screeched from the amount of power he poured into them trying to break the beast's hold. The thing wasn't just insanely strong though, it had the leverage to keep from getting loose and let the other beasts get at him. Together they hammered the torso of his X2 with a barrage of blows. Paul's tactical display died as numerous alarms flashed into existence before his eyes replacing it. His ears were filled with the klaxon blaring warnings his X2 was giving him. Its systems were being damaged with each blow that smashed into it. There wasn't a damned thing Paul could do about it either without figuring out a way to escape the beast that held him.

Dave popped his X2's combat blade. The beast towering above tried to step back out of the weapon's reach but wasn't fast enough. Dave sliced its right leg in two at the knee. Howling, the beast fell sideways. Dave rolled, following it. He drove the sword downward into the beast's chest. The white, hair-covered body of the beast lurched, jerking as the cold alloy of the blade pierced its heart. Dave stood up yanking his combat blade free. He heard the horrible clanging of Paul's X2 being hammered brutally by the other beasts.

"Hey!" Dave shouted through his X2's external speaker instead of over the commlink. His intent was to draw the beasts away from Paul. He instantly regretted it as the world spun before his eyes. Dave realized that he was in shock from the loss of his hand and losing a huge amount of blood. The suit had no means of treating his blown apart hand inside of it beyond shooting him up with meds and that system was apparently offline, disabled somehow by all his X2 had been put through. The pain was seeping through the adrenaline-induced haze his mind was in.

The three beasts around Paul dropped him. Paul's X2 fell with a thud and lay still in the snow. Dave couldn't get through the beasts to check on him. It was going to likely take more than he had left just to survive the next few minutes. The only weapon Dave had was his gore-covered combat sword which dripped red onto the white at his feet.

The power of his X2 began to flick on and off. There were sharp crackling sounds each time it did. Dave was just lucid enough to know that meant he was even more fragged than he had thought. The smoothness of his X2's movement was gone, replaced by an awkward jerking.

None of the beasts had rushed him yet. They were circling him as if looking for an opening. Clearly the things had learned not to underestimate the X2s. Dave didn't attempt to keep up with all three of them. Their motion around him was already turning his stomach without trying to match it. His back exposed and flanks vulnerable as well, Dave could only stand his ground and wait for the beasts to make their move. Bile rose up his throat but Dave swallowed it forcefully down. His skin was slick with a sickly sweat. The remains of his right hand throbbed with each beat of his heart. He could feel the blood continuing to flow from it. It was a miracle that his combat sword had popped and was functional given the amount of damage the machine gun exploding had done to that arm. So far the sword was hanging in there. It hadn't torn off or come loose yet. Dave was seriously beginning to feel that no matter what he did next his life was about to come to an end. He would be going home in a body bag. . .if at all.

The beasts closed in as one, each grabbing for a different part of his armor. One beast snatched a hold of his combat sword, snapping it back and off his suit's arm. Another lunged, trying to tackle him. Dave was able to meet that beast with a clenched metal fist to its face. The thing's nose was crushed to a bloody pulp and driven up into its head. The blow stopped it from taking him over, sending the beast staggering away. The remaining beast was the one behind him. Surging forward, its thick fingers encircled his X2's head, bending it backwards to the point of tearing loose. Dave's own head went with it. Blood geysered up and out of the stump of his neck between the X2's armored shoulders.

An explosion sounded in the distance. The beasts, seeing that Dave was truly dead, forgot about Paul where he lay and raced away in the direction the blast had come from.

Paul had no idea what was happening. All of his X2's systems were dead. He couldn't get any of them to respond through the neural link. Hell, he couldn't even feel the neural link anymore. The suit was too heavy for him to even lift an arm without power. He could wiggle a bit inside of it but that was it. Something must have drawn the beasts away. That was all he could figure or surely they would be trying to rip their way into his X2 to get at him. All he could hear was the occasional pop and hiss of something shorting out or of a dangling wire touching metal. Paul was thankful the suits didn't run on conventional fuel. If they did, his suit would have gone up in flames already.

For now the interior of his X2 was warm and comfortable. That wouldn't last. Without power it wouldn't take too long for him to freeze to death inside his armor. The combat suit had essentially become a metal tomb. A skilled and experienced pilot might have known something that could have been done to either restore the suit's power or somehow manually open the armor to escape it.

Paul's entire knowledge of the X2 combat suits though was a simple crash course in how to use it in combat. He didn't blame Sergeant Hall for not thinking to show those she sent out to fight the beasts what to do if the X2s lost power. She was only human after all and couldn't think of everything. Besides, had any of them really, truly believed that the beasts were as powerful as they were? Paul doubted it. There was nothing to do and nothing that could be done. With a heavy sigh, Paul closed his eyes and let unconsciousness claim him. It would be a peaceful death now and that was more than most in his line of work could ask for.

****

Brewster and Tristan trudged through the ice and snow in silence. The two of them didn't have a lot in common. One a professional soldier, the other a geeky engineer. And that was okay. They didn't need to be friends. They just needed to work together to find and kill the monsters. That was enough. Besides, Tristan was lost playing with the systems of his X2 and Brewster was busy trying not to lose the trail of tracks the two of them had come across and were attempting to follow.

"I still can't get anyone on the comm.,"Tristan blurted out loudly.

The sudden breaking of the silence made

Brewster flinch.

"Dang, man," Brewster shuddered inside his X2. "Can you give me maybe some warning before you get all excited next time?"

Tristan sputtered, "Uh, sure."

"Now what do you mean you can't reach anyone?" Brewster asked.

"Back a ways a bit, I thought it might be a good idea to check in with the others, you know, maybe set up a group link so we all know exactly how the others are doing. I couldn't get through to anyone though," Tristan explained, "So I began to wonder if something was wrong with my armor. Been running diagnostics since then but everything with my X2 is green."

"Okay," Brewster was mildly interested but contacting the other squads right now wasn't a priority for him.

"You don't get it, do you?" The head of Tristan's X2 shook.

"I guess I don't, Tristan," Brewster admitted. "Does it matter though? We all knew we'd be cut off from each other out here and heading in different directions."

"What I am saying, Brewster, is that either there's something out here messing with the comms or the others just aren't responding," Tristan waited for that last bit to sink into

Brewster's head.

"Are you trying to tell me that you think the others are dead or something, Tristan?" Brewster huffed.

"Could be," Tristan said, "Or maybe they just found the creatures, engaged them, and their suits got damaged. . .but most likely whatever it is, it's more than just damage to their suits. The odds of all of them losing their comms in a fight are next to nothing. It's much more likely that either they're all dead or like I said something out here is preventing us from making contact with them."

"What would do that?" Brewster asked.

"Atmospheric interference of some kind, maybe huge deposits of something magnetic in these mountains, some sort of natural EM field, could be a great number of things," Tristan told him., "At this point, there's no means of knowing for sure."

"Right," Brewster tried to keep the frustration he felt out of his voice. "Look, Tristan. I'll give you that it's concerning but we've got a job to do and that's where our focus needs to be."

He heard Tristan mutter something over their shared comm. link.

"Let's just keep moving," Brewster urged. "If a good snowfall comes rolling in, we're going to lose the trail we're following."

Tristan didn't argue. The two of them marched

on in silence once more. Time seemed to pass so slowly that it felt as if they weren't getting anywhere. Everything around appeared to stay pretty much the same, trees, ice, snow. . .

As they approached what appeared to be a much denser area of the woods ahead, Brewster came to a halt and held up a fist signaling for Tristan to do the same.

"What is it?" Tristan yelped. "Do you see something in there?"

"Shush," Brewster barked.

Though he couldn't explain what or why, every one of his instincts told Brewster that something was wrong. It felt like they had just blundered into some kind of trap without realizing it.

A thunderous roar broke the silence from behind where he and Tristan stood. At that same moment, a group of white haired monsters came charging out of the more heavily wooded area ahead of them. Brewster knew the tech with him wasn't up to fending off such a carefully planned ambush. All Brewster could do was try to give Tristan direction as to what needed to be done and hope for the best.

"Tristan!" Brewster yelled. "Take the ones behind us and keep them off of me!'

Brewster's X2 was carrying an automatic combat shotgun. The weapon was insanely powerful but best at close range. Though it took all his willpower, Brewster held his fire as the beasts emerging from the woods charged at him. He waited until they were well clear of the trees and only yards away before letting loose on them. His combat shotgun erupted in a rapid series of clapping booms that would have deafened him, blowing out his ear drums, if not for the noise suppression system of his X2. The heavy rounds it spat ripped the torsos of the two closest to shreds in a wet explosion of red gore that splattered over him and the other beasts around them. The rapid fire blasts also caught several of the others with scattered rounds. One went straight through an eight foot tall beast's leg. The monster went down clutching at the hole left in its wake. Another beast lost most of its right shoulder in a spray of hot blood that steamed in the frigid air. Brewster had done a hell of a lot of damage fast but at the cost of expending the combat shotgun's full magazine. It wasn't enough to cause the remaining beasts to fall back or slow down though. Flipping the weapon around in his armored hands, Brewster swung it like a club. Its butt smashed across the face of a beast, snapping the thing's nose and displacing it sideways. The beast's forward momentum was halted. Before it could recover, Brewster struck again, bringing the shotgun back round to hammer into the beast's face again. This time the beast's jaw was broken with the sickening crack of splintering bone. Upon this second blow the butt of the shotgun crumbled too. As the beast staggered away from him, blood running from its nose and flowing over its black lips, another leaped at Brewster.

Tristan's X2 was packing the standard issue, tri-barrel machine gun. Its barrels whined as they turned and began to spin. He was scared out of his mind. The sight of over a dozen, white, hair-covered, snarling monsters racing towards him almost made him poop his pants. As the tri-barrel became a blazing engine of destruction, he sucked in a breath, getting a tiny shred of his nerves back. His stream of fire cut a swathe of carnage across the frontline of the beasts. Flesh gave way to piercing bullets that tore and mauled the chests of the beasts. Tristan swung the tri-barrel from side to side making sure all of the beasts got some of what he was dishing out. Several fell, shrieking, into the snow. Others plowed onward ignoring the pain and wounds being inflicted upon them. Tristan wanted to run. Just to give up the battle though it had barely begun and get the hell away from the monsters, put as much distance between them and himself as he could. He knew the speeds the X2 suits were capable of if pushed to their max. and didn't think that the beasts could keep up. Tristan was self aware enough to know exactly how much of a coward he was. . .and the fact that he hadn't run already spoke volumes. As scary as facing off against the beasts was, doing it alone would be even worse. That was why he stood his ground and covered Brewster's rear. When Brewster finished with the beasts that had engaged him, Tristan was hoping to hell that the professional soldier was coming to save him. Though it was incredibly stupid and Tristan knew it, he couldn't help but risk a hurried glance over his shoulder in Brewster's direction.

"Brewster!" Tristan wailed, "A little help over here!"

A grunt came over the comm link they shared. Brewster's X2 was grappling with a massive beast. Their arms were locked like wrestlers, each struggling to get the upper hand. Twisting his X2's torso to the right, Brewster managed to hurl the beast from him. The mini machine gun on his suit's arm slid out. Brewster aimed it into the face of the next beast bounding through the snow, rage in its burning eyes. The mini machine gun chattered, spraying fully automatic fire. Bullets punched into the beast's mouth, cheeks, and forehead. One of the beast's eyes exploded to pulp inside of its socket as a round struck it. The beast kept coming. It rammed into Brewster's X2 with such force that it was lifted from the ground and sent flying. Brewster grunted in shock and pain as his X2 landed roughly on its back with a loud, metallic thud. The beast didn't let up. It was on him before Brewster was able to recover, slashing at his X2 with its claws. Sparks flew as they scraped over its metal. The beast howled in fury from not being able to get through the armor at him. Brewster raised his X2's right arm, angling the mini machine gun there to get a shot at the beast. The creature, having been blasted by the weapon already, knew what he was doing. A white, hair-covered hand grabbed his right arm. Brewster struggled to tear it from the beast's grasp. The monster was just too strong. Holding his arm, the beast's other hand reached to take hold of the mini machine gun. With the screech of tearing metal the weapon was ripped away and flung into the distant trees.

Brewster was jarred intensely inside his X2 again as the beast backhanded its head, cracking the faceplate in front of his eyes. The blow hammered him back against the ground and hurt his neck like hell. Brewster knew using the missile in his suit's left arm was out of the question. With the beast right on top of him, he would be blowing himself up too if he did. The only other option left to him was the suit's combat sword. Out of desperation, he popped the weapon. The sword deployed but with the beast still right on him, it merely caught the suit's right arm, forcing it down to prevent being struck by it. Brewster poured power into the arm, pushing the suit to its limits, but still wasn't able to raise the sword. The beast continued to hold it roughly in place against the ground. With its free hand, the beast delivered another blow to the head of his X2. The faceplate wasn't able to withstand another such strike. It shattered raining shards of glass into Brewster's eyes. They closed as quickly as he could make them but it wasn't quick enough. Brewster cried out as tiny bits of glass slashed at his eyes beneath their lids. He didn't see the fingers of the white haired hand as they sunk through the busted faceplate. Fingers closed around the sides of his head inside the X2 and with almost supernatural strength popped his head like a rotten melon. Brewster's brains squirted from his fracturing and cracking skull to splash over the interior of the X2. His body bucked and thrashed, spasming in death, before finally ceasing to lie motionless. The beast flung its head back in a victorious roar.

Tristan's tri-barrel had cut down the bulk of the monsters charging him. Those its deadly spray of high powered rounds didn't kill had veered away from him, rushing for cover as best they could.

According to the data his X2 was feeding him, the weapon was now nearly empty. He wouldn't be able to make such a stand a second time. No help had come from Brewster despite him calling out for it. Tristan popped both the mini missile launcher on his left arm and the machine gun imbedded in his right. As ready as he could be for whatever was coming next, Tristan turned to see what had become of Brewster. His stomach rolled and gurgled, threatening to heave up its contents, as Tristan saw one of the beasts sitting atop Brewster's X2. The beast reached in through the shattered faceplate of Brewster's suit to scoop out something Tristan figured had to be a handful of brains, ramming the gory mess into its mouth.

"Oh frag no," Tristan muttered, raising his left arm. He fired his single shot missile launcher targeting the beast feeding on Brewster. The beast didn't have time to react to Tristan's sudden attack. At most the beast's eyes began to widen before the missile stabbed into its chest like a spear and then exploded. The beast flew apart in a shower of splattering organs and blown off limbs.

Tristan's mind was reeling. Knowing that he couldn't afford not to be concentrating on his surroundings Tristan, through sheer force of will, made himself look around for more of the beasts nearby. And there were more of the things. Those he'd driven off were returning and others were pouring out of the trees beyond where Brewster's savaged X2 was sprawled out in the snow. Tristan knew he couldn't stand and fight. The beasts were too strong and too numerous.

The beasts coming at him from both his front and rear roared and snarled as Tristan darted away to the right. The armored legs of his X2 pumped, all of the suit's power that he could manage pouring into them. The X2's footfalls threw up clods of ice-riddled dirt with each step. The two groups of beasts met and merged, chasing after him. Tristan let out an excited whoop as the beasts didn't appear to be able to keep up. Machine was triumphing over nature. He likely would have escaped too had not the left foot of his X2 come down on a patch of ice so thick that it wasn't able to punch through. That foot slipped out from under Tristan. His X2 shot up from the ground, heels over head, and then crashed down.

"Arr-ugh," Tristan grunted, bouncing around inside of the small pilot space of the armor. His knees slammed into the armor covering them sending pain coursing up his legs. Tristan's head snapped back, banging into the metal behind it and stabbing the neural link that connected him to the X2 poking into the rear of his neck. It didn't pierce through but the added pain from it was enormous and nearly made him lose consciousness. Vision blurred and head throbbing, Tristan saw that the X2 itself hadn't taken any damage from the unexpected fall.

Tristan's X2 rolled over and scrambled onto its feet. The beasts had caught up to him in the fleeting moments it took for him to fall and get up. The first of them swung a clenched fist that smashed in the faceplate of his X2. Glass gave way, shattering, and spraying inward over Tristan. Thankfully none of it got in his eyes. It did pockmark his cheeks and forehead with dots of red where the glass imbedded itself in his skin.

Howling like an enraged banshee, Tristan caught the beast's arm and brought it down at the same time he raised one of the legs of his X2 under it, snapping the bone through the thick muscle that surrounded it. The beast shrieked and yanked free of his hold on it. Tristan followed up with a high kick to the beast's chest that knocked the beast off its feet. He would have finished the creature there and then but two more were already within reach, black lips parted with snarls of primal rage. He moved fast to parry a blow from the one that came at him from his right as the one coming from the left raised both hands, clenched together, above its head to bring down towards Tristan's shoulder. Hustling it to the side, he dodged the double handed swing and countered by kicking out at that beast. He didn't aim high. Tristan needed the damn thing down and out of commission as much as he could make it. His armored foot met the beast's knee, smashing it. The beast, no longer having a right leg that would support its weight, fell sideways into the snow. Tristan's attention was drawn to the other beast as it roared and took another swing at him, this time with its claws. He backpedaled just enough so that only the tips of the claws raked across the front of his X2's armored chest. Two of the beast's claws were torn away as they dragged over the metal there. Ignoring the pain and reversing its swing, the beast's hand met the head of Tristan's X2 with a vicious backhanded slap. Tristan's ears rang inside the X2. The impact stunned him giving the beast a chance to do more damage. Its massive hand latched onto the side of the X2's head and twisted. Sparks burst out as several systems went offline. The beast was unable to wrench the X2's, and Tristan's head along with it, off. Tristan shoved the X2's arms up between the beast's and thrust them apart, swinging his head forward. Metal met bone once more. The beast stumbled backwards, giving Tristan room to breathe but the action cost him dearly. His X2 slumped forward onto its knees as Tristan strained not to pass out. His ears were still ringing and the world was swimming around him before his eyes. Black flecks spotted his vision like dark stars.

Using every last bit of his strength and will, Tristan's X2 righted itself blocking yet another blow that hurled towards him from the beast on his other flank. He popped his X2's combat sword and slashed wildly at that beast. It was on the ground next to him still unable to stand because of what he'd done to its knee. The blade caught the beast just above its groin and slashed upwards to its sternum. The white hair and skin beneath it split like an opening maw. Purple, red-slicked coils of intestines unfurled, pouring out. The beast's exposed innards steamed in the frigid cold of the air. The beast's mouth opened as if it was trying to scream like a human would but only a mouthful of bright red blood emerged from it. The wet red splashed over its chin onto the white of its chest. Grunting with effort, Tristan freed the blade from the beast's body and then heaved his X2 onto its feet.

The other beast had recovered. Its nose was a mashed mess of collapsed and fractured bone at the center of its face and blood leaked from its remains. The beast was utterly enraged, even more so than before. Tristan backed away from it, surprised the creature wasn't already attacking him. Instead, it stood, eyes burning with anger, watching his X2.

As if waking up from a dream, Tristan realized just how many more beasts surrounded the two of them. Dozens of the monsters were lined about him and the beast with the crushed nose, in a circle blocking any chance of escape. It didn't make a bit of sense. The things should have overpowered him and torn his X2 apart. They easily could have, given their numbers. It was as if they were letting the single beast within the circle with him have a shot at taking him out on its own. The apparent intelligence of the beasts made Tristan shudder.

Breathing raggedly through its mashed mess of a nose, the beast in the circle with him lurched forward. Tristan moved to meet it. His combat sword flashed through the air. Its tip sliced a red groove across the beast's chest. Spitting out a mouthful of blood, the beast grabbed the blade of the sword on its back swing. With a quick motion, its huge hands ripped the blade off the arm of Tristan's X2. Tristan hastily retreated as much as he could. The snarls of the beasts in the circle behind him limited his movement. He was terrified to get too close to them for the fear that they would join the fight before he'd finished the beast he was engaged with. The beast rushed forward again. Tristan's X2 sunk, dipping, before springing into the air, legs launching it upwards. Like some sort of warped kung fu robot, the X2 came back down, the fist of its right hand striking the beast on its already smashed nose. The center of the beast's face collapsed inward, driven by the force of the metal ramming into it. The X2's hand sunk deep into the beast's head killing it instantly. Tristan panicked as he was unable to tug his armored hand from the beast's skull.

A series of growls arose from the beasts surrounding him. As one they swarmed his X2. Claws tried to dig into alloy steel. Grasping fingers pulled and tugged. Alarm klaxons blared loudly in Tristan's ears. Sparks flew as circuits blew. Metal gave way to rage. One arm was torn away and then the other, Tristan's with them, blood spurting. Tristan wailed like a maniac. His cries could be heard through the X2's external speakers. They drove the beasts on in their mad attack. The creatures lifted Tristan's X2, fighting over it, as they ripped away its legs and head. Tristan died screaming, blood and mechanical fluids splashing over the snow-covered ground.

****

Harry ran the fingers of his right hand through his gray speckled and thinning hair. There was a sharp throbbing in his back between his shoulders. Any other time Harry would have worried that he might be having a heart attack. Right now though, his worries were all concentrated on Tristan. His friend and fellow engineer had ventured out of the Z56 hours ago accompanying the soldiers and Mason, the transport's remaining pilot, who had been sent to kill the monsters that were lurking in the woods beyond the clearing where the Z56 crashed. His wife told him over and over about how bad a habit rubbing at his hair was and that it only sped up the baldness that was beginning atop his head. Harry didn't give a crap. At his age, some things were just written into the stone of how he lived and there was no way to change them. He told himself that anyway.

Harry sat in the briefing room that was being used as the Z56's C.I.C. along with Sergeant Hall and Lieutenant Lane. Sergeant Hall paced nervously while the lieutenant simply leaned back in his chair at the head of the table, frowning. They had lost contact with all three of the two man, X2 squads well over an hour ago. It was impossible to know if there was something out there blocking their communications or if those dispatched to slay the beasts had instead been eliminated themselves. Harry feared the latter was true. It would certainly fit the luck they all had been cursed with since the Z56 flew into the atmospheric storm that brought it down.

Sergeant Hall stopped her pacing and stood

glaring at Lieutenant Lane.

"Just how much longer are we gonna wait until we start doing something?" she challenged him. "We can't just sit here."

Lieutenant Lane, while knowing she was right, merely shrugged, "And what exactly would you have us be doing, Sergeant? We've already secured the Z56 as much as we possibly can. Every single person aboard is armed and well aware that those things could be coming for us at any moment."

"Frag it,"Sergeant Hall spat, "I don't know but we should be doing something."

Harry spoke up, surprising himself that he had the courage to do it. "We're all exhausted and emotionally on edge. Maybe what we should be doing is getting our emotions, our fear, better under control before we decide about anything else."

"If Brewster and the rest are dead. . ." Sergeant Hall shook her head, an expression of hopelessness on her attractive, sharp features,"then there are damn few of us left to do anything."

"No freaking kidding," Lieutenant Lane snorted. "And it's all on me. Not you. Not him," he gestured at Harry, "But me. I took over for the colonel and now. . ."

"Stop it," Sergeant Hall snapped. "You're not allowed to think like that! For better or worse, you're the commanding officer here and you can't be beating yourself up over crap until we make it out of here alive."

"She's right," Harry nodded.

"Oh what the hell," Lieutenant Lane shrugged. "We're likely all dead anyway."

"When exactly did you become a quitter, LT?" Sergeant Hall was scowling.

"I guess the moment we all ended up in some sicko, psychotic horror movie," Lieutenant Lane said, "Those damn monsters don't have any right to even exist."

"Well get your crap together. . .sir," Sergeant Hall ordered in her best drill sergeant voice. "We need you to get your head out of your butt and lead us."

"So who do we have left?" Harry cut in, "I mean aside from the three of us."

"Rigdon is watching the cargo bay door. Joe is guarding the lower emergency exit under the pilot compartment. I've got Tyler up in the cockpit, freezing and hating life, keeping an eye out up there," Lieutenant Lane answered. "Oh and Tony's in sick bay doing his thing."

"Seven," Sergeant Hall moaned, "Seven of us left."

"And none of your power suits Sergeant," Harry reminded them both.

Sergeant Hall shook her head. "I'm not ready to concede that just yet. I just can't accept that those things out there could have taken on combat suits as advanced as the X2s and won."

"Clearly something's happened out there," Harry's brow creased as he frowned.

"People," Lieutenant Lane would have hopped up from his seat if he could have but his injured leg prevented that. It was hurting worse it seemed with every passing hour. "None of this is getting us anywhere."

Sergeant Hall watched Lane intently hoping he was finally stepping up again.

"Don't look at me like that, Hall," Lieutenant Lane told her. "I haven't come up with some miracle plan out of the blue but you're both right. We have to do something. What about you, Harry? You have any ideas?"

"What I've got is more bad news," Harry sighed. "The power isn't going to last much longer. I'd say we're down to a few more hours at best. The cold is playing havoc with what Tristan and I rigged up as well as draining the batteries."

"Can you give the comm. systems another look and see if maybe there's anything you can do to get a message out?" Sergeant Hall asked.

"Sure, I can look," Harry didn't bother arguing though they all knew that particular route was a dead end.

"Anything else possible that could buy us more juice to keep the heat going?" Sergeant Hall walked closer to Harry and leaned onto the table between where he and Lieutenant Lane sat.

"Not a damn thing," Harry gritted his teeth.

"How long do you think we'll have when it goes?" Sergeant Hall pressed the engineer.

"That's more of a question for Tony," Harry wanted to roll his eyes but didn't. "He's the medic. I work with machines remember?"

"Even with the residual heat inside the Z56," Lieutenant Lane guessed, "I'd think we would have less than a day as cold as it is up here."

"That's a pretty grim estimate," Harry rose up from his seat.

"Where are you going?" Lieutenant Lane eyed him.

"To check over the communications systems again," Harry huffed, barely able to keep from snapping due to the extreme frustration he was sure they were all feeling, not just him. "I thought. . ."

"Yeah, yeah," Lieutenant Lane waved him on. "Go on. Get it done."

As Harry moved towards the exit leading towards the front of the plane, a frantic voice came through the short range comms they all were wearing.

"Lieutenant! Rigdon shouted. "Those things. . .they're here!"

The echo of huge fists hammering on the metal of the cargo bay door could be heard in the background as Rigdon was yelling.

****

Tyler shivered as a cold wind blew the broken forward window. The damn thing had only been cracked from the crash but the frigid temps and pressure of the weight from the snow piling up on top of the compartment finished the job. Hell, that was just a guess. Tyler didn't really know what made the window finally crumble and he supposed it didn't really matter. Pulling his parka tighter around him, Tyler sighed, watching his breath in the air.

When Tyler joined the military, if being honest with himself, he'd wanted adventure, a sense of purpose, and to become a hero. There were none of those things here. The plane had crashed through some sort of accident, not battling evil. He was almost certainly going to die in these snowy hills and for no other reason than bad luck. And even if he gave his life to save those others of his unit left alive, would it matter? In the end, deep down, Tyler figured they would die too. The odds weren't just stacked against them all, they were overwhelming. It was horrid to think such thoughts but they were the truth of how things stood.

Tyler dug a cigarette from a pocket and lit up. He inhaled deeply, letting the smoke fill his lungs before breathing it out. His eyes came to rest on the glowing ember at the cigarette's end. It only served to remind him how cold he was. If it were up to him, he and the other survivors would be hanging in the warmest part of the Z56 they could find and drinking away their last hours. Hours? Yeah, that sounded right. If those beasts had really taken down six heavily armored war machines like the X2 suits that meant the rest of them were screwed. It was only a matter of time until those things came for them and given that they knew exactly where they were, Tyler didn't think it would take long for them to make their move. Animals don't sit around making plans or brooding like humans. No. They were coming and it would be sooner rather than later.

Holding his M4A1 so tightly that his knuckles were white and with his cigarette dangling from his lips, Tyler moved closer to the shattered forward window of the pilot compartment. The sun was beginning to set and the shadows among the trees in the distance were long and dark. Tyler was well aware that the pilot compartment was the most vulnerable part of the Z56. When the beasts came, this was the one spot that they would surely breach the huge transport through. His job was to see them well enough in advance to get the interior doors beyond it sealed behind him to keep them from breaching further and warn the others of what was happening. There was a decent amount of clear ground between the Z56's nose and the woods. He should be able to see the things easily when they made their move. Should. That was the operative word. Tyler vividly remembered an old movie about Bigfoot he'd seen as a kid. The name of it escaped him but in it the Sasquatch was able to either refract light somehow or bend a human's preceptions of it so that the beast appeared to somewhere that it wasn't or at least obscure its presence so only those with the keenest of senses knew it was there. Tyler hoped the things outside couldn't do that too. The damned things had enough advantages already.

Even squinting, Tyler didn't see anything but snow and distant trees. He took a final drag from his cigarette and allowed it to fall from his lips to the floor of the compartment. With a slight movement of a booted foot, Tyler ground it out. That single instant was all it took. His guard was down and his attention away from the forward window. A massive, white form burst into the pilot compartment right in front of him. It hadn't come from the direction he'd been looking earlier. The thing had come across the body of the plane above where he stood and came downward into and through the window. The thing must have crawled, slowly, silently, to take him utterly by surprise as it had.

Leaping backwards to put some space between himself and the monster, Tyler swung the barrel of his M4A1 up. He squeezed the rifle trigger. The M4A1 blazed on full auto, spent round casings clattering to the floor from it. The monster in front of Tyler stood eight feet tall. Its head had to be tilted slightly forward to avoid hitting the ceiling of the compartment. Its eyes burned with a feral and primal hunger. The bullets Tyler fired cut a swathe of red from its sternum towards the bottom of its neck. The beast's reaction was fierce and blindingly fast. Its massive hand shot forward to snatch the barrel of the rifle, bending it beneath the force of its grip. Tyler let the creature tear the weapon from his grasp, drawing the Glock 19 holstered on his hip. He didn't have any faith that pistol would stop the monster but it was all he had.

Flinging the bent M4A1 away into the wall of the pilot compartment, the monster advanced on Tyler. He continued to backpedal towards the compartment's exit. He desperately wanted to just turn and make a run for it. His instincts told Tyler that he would be dead if he did. The thing was too fast. It was like lightning despite its size and bulk.

Tyler's Glock cracked in rapid succession as he popped off a series of shots aiming for the white haired monster's eyes. All of his rounds missed their mark as the thing jerked its head to the right. The bullets struck the beast's cheek and jaw. Blood splashed from where they hit. One punched through softer flesh finding its way inside the monster's mouth. It spat the round and a glob of bloody saliva out. Tyler flinched as the monster gave a roar that echoed off the walls of the compartment around them, so loud that his ears rang in its wake. He nearly dropped his Glock from the pain of it.

The monster lunged at him, a clawed hand swiping through the air that passed by his face only mere fractions of an inch from tearing away his nose. Tyler sucked in a sharp breath as he realized his retreat had finally taken him through the compartment's exit. He slammed a hand onto the control that shut the door between it and the corridor he now stood in. The door shut with a banging clang. The monster on the other side of it struck the door with such force it visibly dented outward before Tyler's eyes. There was no chance in hell that it would hold long against the beast's rage.

Activating his comm. Tyler shouted, "We've been breached in the pilot compartment! I repeat, we've been breached!"

Tyler died as the door gave way and flew into the corridor. It pushed Tyler into the wall behind him. The beast continued to press on it as Tyler's pained screams became sickening gargles and then quickly fell silent. Tyler's bones snapped upon themselves, flesh compacting, until he burst like an over aired balloon, the blood and other fluids of his body splashing everywhere.

****

Tony heard Tyler's warning over the comm. Joe's came next only seconds later.

"They've broken in at my position too!" Joe yelled, pure terror in his voice. "The things kept ramming into the bulkhead door until it gave enough for a group of them to be able to get a good grip on it and then they tore it away like the top of a can of spam!"

The lieutenant's voice responded. "Can you hold them, Joe?"

The shrieks of a dying man were what came back in answer to the lieutenant's question.

Rigdon's voice cut in. "The cargo bay is clear! I repeat, the cargo bay is clear! The bastards aren't able to get through back here! I'm abandoning this post and moving forward to help!"

If the lieutenant was angered by Rigdon's choice, he said nothing about it. The comm. went as silent as it had been before all hell broke loose. Tony looked down to see that his hands were shaking so bad he could barely hold onto the medical bag he'd been packing.

A low, guttural growl drew his attention to the door leading out of the sick bay. Tony's eyes bugged as he saw the creature standing there. It stood over seven feet tall, all muscle and white hair. What Tony found himself staring at though was its mouth. Yellow, fanged teeth gleamed in the dim, failing light of the sick bay, and blood smeared the hair above and below its black lips that were parted in a fierce snarl. Tony felt his bladder release itself. A warm current ran over the curves of his legs, soaking his pants, and pooling at his feet.

The beast strolled into the bay with him. Its stride was calm as if it knew that there was no way out except through it. Tony's only weapon was a Glock 19 strapped in a holster on his left hip. The medical bag he held slipped from his hands to thud onto the floor sending urine splashing. His left hand went for the Glock. The monster rushed up to catch his wrist as the pistol cleared its holster. The bones in his wrist crunched as Tony wailed. With a twist, the monster tore away his hand clutching the

Glock and the weapon with it. Blood spurted from the stump as Tony jerked away trying to escape any more violence. There was a small medical table close by and he shoved at the beast, attempting to block its path to him as he continued to stumble towards the sick bay's rear wall. Flinging the table over effortlessly, the beast cornered Tony. This time there was nowhere to go and nothing to fight back with. Not that it mattered, Tony was pretty much spent. The shock and blood loss had him skittering the edge of unconsciousness. His vision was blurred and dark floaters danced before his eyes. Tony's breath came as ragged gasps. He looked up at the great beast as it closed the distance to tower over him.

"Ple. . .Please," Tony stammered. "Please let me go."

A white, hair-covered hand took him by the throat, lifting Tony from the floor, pressing his back up against the wall and holding him there. Tony's legs thrashed wildly and his right hand clawed at the beast's hand that held him. The beast's other hand raised so that the claw of its pointer finger found the hollow dip of the flesh of his throat. Its tip pricked his skin. The beast gave a series of pleasured huffs shoving its finger deeper. Hot liquid filled Tony's mouth and began to choke him. It was his own blood. His kicking became even more frantic as he could no longer breathe. Then the beast slashed downward with its finger. Tony opened up from where the finger had entered him to just above his groin. His chest and abdomen turned into an opening maw, pressed outward by the weight of the organs no longer held within him. Coils of purple intestines in a mess of gushing red splattered onto the floor beneath his body.

The beast leaned closer, sniffing at Tony, and then let go of his corpse. It turned and walked out of the sick bay in search of more prey.

****

Harry was supposed to have been working on the long range comms when the invasion of the Z56 by the beasts began. That wasn't what he had been up to at all. After leaving his meeting with Lieutenant Lane and Sergeant Hall, Harry had headed straight for the huge transport's central fuel supply. Sweat dripped from Harry's brow from his efforts at rigging the Z56 to blow at his command. Losing Tristan, he knew his friend was dead out there somewhere, was the final straw that broke the last of his hopes of making it home alive. The detonator Harry finished rigging would create a blast that would tear the entire transport apart in flames. He wiped at the dripping sweat with the back of his hand as the chaos erupted over the comm. The beasts were inside the Z56 now. He wasn't a soldier. He was an engineer, a tech. There wasn't a damn thing he could do to stop the things so Harry stayed right where he was, detonator clutched to his chest like a holy relic that could provide his salvation.

Mere moments later, he wasn't startled at all to see Lieutenant Lane and Sergeant Hall entering the central engineering section. Sergeant Hall skidded to a halt just inside the doorway, turning to fire the pump action shotgun in her hands at something beyond it. The blast echoed in the wide room.

"Get the hell up, Harry, and help us secure this section, man!" Lieutenant Lane barked.

Harry only smiled weakly. "Afraid it's too late for that."

On the other side of the engineering section several white, hair-covered monsters were already pouring through the doorway there.

Sergeant Hall saw what Harry was holding. She sprinted towards him in a desperate attempt to knock it from him.

"Don't you dare. . ." She raged but never got to finish her sentence because Harry triggered the detonator he held.

The huge form of the Z56 bucked, rocked by an explosion at its center. Secondary explosions boomed along the length of the transport in both directions. Flames leaped skyward and chunks of twisted, scorched metal were flung everywhere. Dozens upon dozens of beasts gathered around it died. The few that weren't caught directly by the blast were set on fire as flaming fuel rained over them. Shrieking they ran about, howling as their hair was burned away, their skin bubbling, and fatty tissues sizzling.

Epilogue

Mason and Samuel trudged to the top of the small hill at the edge of the clearing partially created by the Z56's crash.

"My God. . ."Mason gasped.

Samuel was apparently struck speechless by the sight ahead of them.

The shattered remains of the Z56 were burning. Streams of billowing smoke rose skyward. All around the remnants of the transport lay the smoldering corpses of too many beasts for Mason to count at a glance. In the light of the flames he could see the blackened, crisp flesh of their bodies. There were a few of the creatures that were still alive. . .but they were dying. Cranking up the audio sensitivity of his X2, Mason could hear their moans.

"Everyone's dead," Samuel said, so deadpan that it was obvious he was in shock."They have to be."

Mason didn't argue the statement. It looked like the beasts had stormed the Z56. The monsters must have broken into the interior of the transport and in a futile, last stand someone aboard had blown the transport up in order to take as many of the things with them as possible.

Sighing, Mason finally responded, "Looks that way."

"Should. . .should we go down there and check?" Samuel asked.

The head of Mason's X2 shook in the negative. "Look at that mess. No one's alive down there. There's no way anyone could have survived an explosion like that. They blew the plane in such a way as to maximize the blast."

"Yeah. . . yeah," Samuel stuttered, "You're right."

"I don't think there's any point in us going down there to finish off the last of those things that are still breathing either," Mason added. "The best thing we can do is get the hell out of here."

"What?" Samuel turned to him.

"We head for the base that we were originally bound for," Mason explained. "With these suits, we might just be able to make it there."

"You really think we can?" Samuel pleaded.

"What else are we gonna do, Sam? Lie down and die?" Mason quipped. "The coordinates of the base are in these suits. All we have to do is put in the legwork."

"Okay," Samuel agreed.

"Let's get moving then," Mason ordered. "Who knows just how long the power in these suits is gonna last in this cold."

Mason led the two of them as they left the burning wreckage of the Z56 behind. The battered X2s marched onward through the night.

Eric S Brown is the author of numerous book series including the Bigfoot War series, the Psi-Mechs Inc. series, the Kaiju Apocalypse series (with Jason Cordova), the Crypto-Squad series (with Jason Brannon), the Jack Bunny Bam series, and the A Pack of Wolves series. Some of his stand alone books include Snarl, Sasquatch Nightmare, Manhunt, Cryptid Park, War of the Worlds plus Blood Guts and Zombies, Casper Alamo (with Jason Brannon), Sasquatch Island, Day of the Sasquatch, Bigfoot, Crashed, World War of the Dead, Last Stand in a Dead Land, Sasquatch Lake, Kaiju Armageddon, Megalodon, Megalodon Apocalypse, Kraken, Alien Battalion, The Last Fleet, and From the Snow They Came to name only a few. His short fiction has been published hundreds of times in the small press in beyond including markets like the Onward Drake and Black Tide Rising anthologies from Baen Books, the Grantville Gazette, the SNAFU Military horror anthology series, and Walmart World magazine. He has done the novelizations for such films as Boggy Creek: The Legend is True (Studio 3 Entertainment) and The Bloody Rage of Bigfoot (Great Lake films). The first book of his Bigfoot War series was adapted into a feature film by Origin Releasing in 2014. Werewolf Massacre at Hell's Gate was the second of his books to be adapted into film in 2015. Major Japanese publisher, Takeshobo, bought the reprint rights to his Kaiju Apocalypse series (with Jason Cordova) and the mass market, Japanese language version was released in late 2017. Ring of Fire Press has released a collected edition of his Monster Society stories (set in the New York Times Best-selling world of Eric Flint's 1632). In addition to his fiction, Eric also wrote a pop culture column featured in Altered Reality Magazine for many years. Eric lives in North Carolina with his wife and two children where he continues to write tales of the hungry dead, blazing guns, and the things that lurk in the woods.

Check out other great

Cryptid Novels!

J.H. Moncrieff

RETURN TO DYATLOV PASS

In 1959, nine Russian students set off on a skiing expedition in the Ural Mountains. Their mutilated bodies were discovered weeks later. Their bizarre and unexplained deaths are one of the most enduring true mysteries of our time. Nearly sixty years later, podcast host Nat McPherson ventures into the same mountains with her team, determined to finally solve the mystery of the Dyatlov Pass incident. Her plans are thwarted on the first night, when two trackers from her group are brutally slaughtered. The team's guide, a superstitious man from a neighboring village, blames the killings on yetis, but no one believes him. As members of Nat's team die one by one, she must figure out if there's a murderer in their midst—or something even worse—before history repeats itself and her group becomes another casualty of the infamous Dead Mountain.

Gerry Griffiths

CRYPTID ZOO

As a child, rare and unusual animals, especially cryptid creatures, always fascinated Carter Wilde. Now that he's an eccentric billionaire and runs the largest conglomerate of high-tech companies all over the world, he can finally achieve his wildest dream of building the most incredible theme park ever conceived on the planet... CRYPTID ZOO. Even though there have been apparent problems with the project, Wilde still decides to send some of his marketing employees and their families on a forced vacation to assess the theme park in preparation for Opening Day. Nick Wells and his family are some of those chosen and are about to embark on what will become the most terror-filled weekend of their lives—praying they survive. STEP RIGHT UP AND GET YOUR FREE PASS... TO CRYPTID ZOO

Check out other great

Cryptid Novels!

P.K. Hawkins

THE CRYPTID FILES

Fresh out of the academy with top marks, Agent Bradley Tennyson is expecting to have the pick of cases and investigations throughout the country. So he's shocked when instead he is assigned as the new partner to "The Crag," an agent well past his prime. He thinks the assignment is a punishment. It's anything but. Agent George Crag has been doing this job for far longer than most, and he knows what skeletons his bosses have in the closet and where the bodies are buried. He has pretty much free reign to pick his cases, and he knows exactly which one he wants to use to break in his new young partner: the disappearance and murder of a couple of college kids in a remote mountain town. Tennyson doesn't realize it, but Crag is about to introduce him to a world he never believed existed: The Cryptid Files, a world of strange monsters roaming in the night. Because these murders have been going on for a long time, and evidence is mounting that the murderer may just in fact be the legendary Bigfoot.

Gerry Griffiths

DOWN FROM
BEAST MOUNTAIN

A beast with a grudge has come down from the mountain to terrorize the townsfolk of Porterville. The once sleepy town is suddenly wide awake. Sheriff Abel McGuire and game warden Grant Tanner frantically investigate one brutal slaying after another as they follow the blood trail they hope will eventually lead to the monstrous killer. But they better hurry and stop the carnage before the census taker has to come out and change the population sign on the edge of town to ZERO.

SEVERED**PRESS**

🐦 @severedpress
f /severedpress

Check out other great
Cryptid Novels!

Hunter Shea
LOCH NESS REVENGE

Deep in the murky waters of Loch Ness, the creature known as Nessie has returned. Twins Natalie and Austin McQueen watched in horror as their parents were devoured by the world's most infamous lake monster. Two decades later, it's their turn to hunt the legend. But what lurks in the Loch is not what they expected. Nessie is devouring everything in and around the Loch, and it's not alone. Hell has come to the Scottish Highlands. In a fierce battle between man and monster, the world may never be the same. Praise for THEY RISE : "Outrageous, balls to the wall...made me yearn for 3D glasses and a tub of popcorn, extra butter!" – The Eyes of Madness "A fast-paced, gore-heavy splatter fest of sharksploitation." The Werd "A rocket paced horror story. I enjoyed the hell out of this book." Shotgun Logic Reviews

C.G. Mosley
BAKER COUNTY
BIGFOOT CHRONICLE

Marie Bledsoe only wants her missing brother Kurt back. She'll stop at nothing to make it happen and, with the help of Kurt's friend Tony, along with Sheriff Ray Cochran, Marie embarks on a terrifying journey deep into the belly of the mysterious Walker Laboratory to find him. However, what she and her companions find lurking in the laboratory basement is beyond comprehension. There are cryptids from the forest being held captive there and something...else. Enjoy this suspenseful tale from the mind of C.G. Mosley, author of Wood Ape. Welcome back to Baker County, a place where monsters do lurk in the night!